THE
TETROMET
TAPES

BY

EZEKIEL KINCAID

D & T
PUBLISHING

To the 1980s and my home town of Central, Louisiana. Thank you for giving me so much material to work with and some incredible urban legends.

THE
TETROMET
TAPES

Central, Louisiana. End
of May, 1990

———————————

Time flowed like shit through a straw for sixth grader Jon Benson. The second hand on the wall clock labored under some invisible force, struggling with every tick. Maybe the batteries are dying, he thought. No way we still have five minutes left! He counted along with the motions of the second hand. One one thousand, two one thousand, three one thousand. His words were in sync with its turning. Maybe I'm just counting slow?

Jon sat at his desk in English class, chewing the end of his pen cap. His hazel eyes burned holes into the clock hanging on the wall at the front of the classroom. His foot tapped the floor with spastic fervor, shoelaces bouncing as clods of dirt from the playground dislodged from the sole of his shoe. Dirty, blond hair perched disheveled on top of his head from the strain of last hour's PE, and the lingering taste of the peanut butter sandwich he ate at lunch was still on his tongue. It was the final minutes of school before summer break, and Jon Benson had reached the end of his patience.

The days of smelling chalk dust and laminated papers would soon be a faint memory. Shitty cafeteria food, sometimes weaved with captive strands of lunch lady hair, would be replaced by outdoor cookouts. Late-night movies and wrestling marathons were on the horizon, along with the summer sun and aroma of freshly cut grass. Pool parties, endless Nintendo time, and evenings of backyard football would replace ringing bells and boring-ass teachers.

"Jon, you having a seizure over there or something?" Bill Chapman sat at the desk next to Jon, staring at him with a smirk. His long, black hair drooped in his face as he talked. "You gotta bleed the old lizard?"

"I think the clock's broken," Jon said.

"Staring at it isn't gonna make the time go by faster," said Bill. "Why don't we annoy Dup?" He motioned with his head towards the front of the class.

Chase Dupuy was a few desks up, to Jon's left. He glanced over at him, and Chase was leaned up out of the seat with his ass in the air. Jen sat in front of him, and he was whispering something in her ear.

"I got a good shot." Jon curled his lip into a half

smile. "Watch this." He reached in his backpack and pulled out a rubber band tied around a pencil.

"What are you gonna do?" Bill leaned in closer.

Jon ripped the eraser off his pencil with his teeth, like he was pulling the pin from a grenade. He then wrapped the rubber band through his fingers, making a miniature slingshot. He spat the eraser in his other hand, cupped it in the band, and pulled back. Jon fired. The pink rubber projectile whizzed through the air and pelted Chase right in the left butt cheek. Chase bolted up with a wince, his wavy, charcoal colored hair bobbing.

"Ah, shit!" Chase pulled away from Jen in a flash. He looked over his shoulder and rubbed his ass. Giggles erupted from behind him. He glanced over at Bill and Jon, who were hee-hawing like a couple of jackasses.

"Chase Dupuy," Mrs. Davis said. The teacher looked up from behind a stack of dog-eared papers in the middle of her desk. She glared at Chase with a wrinkled brow and puckered lips. Mrs. Davis was pushing sixty years old and styled her gray hair like a soft serve ice cream cone. "Language, young man! It would be a shame to send you to the principal's office three minutes before the last day of school ends."

Chase pursed his lips and shook his head. He sat down in his seat and, when Mrs. Davis returned to her papers, flipped Jon and Bill the bird.

"Fuck you, assholes," Chase mouthed.

Jon and Bill laughed harder.

"Bill Chapman and Jon Benson." Mrs. Davis slapped her papers down on the desktop. Three distinct lines appeared across her forehead. Her burning vision cut through the boys like heat rays. "I don't know what is so funny, but I am sure it wouldn't be amusing if you two had to go to the office as well."

"Yes, ma'am," Jon said, giving an apologetic grin. "Sorry."

Mrs. Davis's eyes darted back and forth from Jon and Bill to Chase. Satisfied the little outburst was over, she gathered her papers and went back to reading.

"Little bitch," Jon mouthed at Chase. He held up the rubber band and waved it at him.

Chase snickered and shook his head. "I am gonna …" He made a slicing motion with his finger across his throat.

Jon returned the gesture, except with his middle finger.

The boys went back and forth until a loud metallic ringing interrupted their charades. It was the sound of victory. The bell rang, and all the students leaped out of their desks, grabbing their stuff in a mad frenzy. Cheers and screams resounded, and the pitter patter of sixth grade feet bustled towards the door. Chase grabbed his backpack and ran over to Bill and Jon, who waited for him in the hall.

"Why'd you do that, Jon?" Chase asked. "I was in the middle of putting the moves on Jen." He gave Jon a shove on the shoulder.

The boys walked in stride together to the exit.

"Dup," Bill said. "The only moves you have is whacking it up and down." He held up his fist and made a stroking motion.

"Very funny, Chapman." Chase now gave Bill a slight shove on the shoulder.

"We all hanging out at your house tomorrow evening, Bill?" Jon asked.

"Yep, still the plan."

The boys had cleaned their lockers out earlier, so there was no need to delay their freedom. Jon had even found an old Werewolf by Night comic he had accused Chase of swiping earlier in the year. Since then, Jon stopped bringing important shit to school. Except for today. He gripped the Ken Griffey, Jr. rookie card his dad bought him yesterday. He wanted to show it off to Bill and Chase. Well, rub it in their faces was more like it.

"Hey, check this out," Jon said. He slipped the card from his front pants pocket and waved it at his friends. "Look what I got." It was locked and secured in a plastic protector case.

Bill's eyes almost popped out of their sockets, and Chase made a grab at it.

"Let me see that," Chase said.

Jon yanked the card back. "I'm not letting you touch it. You bent my Jose Canseco rookie card, you turd."

"No I didn't." Chase went for the card again.

Jon slapped his arm away. "The hell you didn't.

Here, Bill." Jon handed the card to Bill.

"Asshole," Chase muttered.

"Sweet," Bill said, inspecting the card. "Upper Deck! No way!"

"Let me see!" Chase reached for the card.

Bill pushed him away. "Get off me, Dup." He handed the card back to Jon. "Where did you get it?"

Jon slipped the card into his front pocket. "Early birthday present from my dad."

"You wanna trade it for anything?" Chase asked. "I've got a Craig Biggio rookie."

Jon curled his upper lip. "No, you idiot."

The boys chuckled at their exchange and neared the exit. Freedom was only about ten yards away. They bolted straight for the door, sneakers squeaking away on the vinyl tiles. Right before they made it outside, a tall girl with flowing blonde hair and piercing blue eyes came out of her classroom. She cut right in front of them, halting their progress. The girl glanced over her shoulder at the trio, a beaming smile on her face.

"Hi, Jon." It was Laurianne Potter.

The boys stopped dead in their tracks. They gazed at Laurianne with goo-goo eyes and gaped mouths. The sunlight shone through the window behind Laurianne, creating a sort of angelic glow all around her.

"Uh, hi." Jon's voice cracked a little, and he gave her a nervous smile.

"Do y'all have any big summer plans?" she asked.

"Um, no. I mean yes … I mean, sort of." Jon looked away and shrugged, his cheeks burning red.

Bill gave him a gentle elbow to the ribs.

"What about you?" Jon tried to play it cool.

"Going to Florida for vacation in July. Maybe we could hang out before I go," Laurianne said.

"That … uh." Jon swallowed and shifted his backpack from shoulder to shoulder. "That would be swell."

Chase and Bill turned their faces away and clenched their jaws shut.

"Yeah, I would like that." Laurianne leaned in and gave Jon a kiss on the cheek.

Jon's cheeks glowed red again, and a Cheshire grin spread across his face.

"Bye," Laurianne said and walked off.

Jon brushed his fingers across his face, the feel of her lips still leaving their impression. His stomach turned, his heartbeat picked up, and his summer just got a hell of a lot brighter.

Bill and Chase caved, and the chuckles erupted.

"Oh God!" Chase snorted. "Yeah, that would be swell," he said, mocking Jon.

Bill joined in. "Swell? Swell? What? This the 1950s? Golly gee, Beave, that would be swell!"

"Make fun all you want," Jon said, vision

cemented on Laurianne in the distance. "Who's the one who got a kiss on the cheek?" His eyebrow raised with his words.

"Hey, fellas, wait up!" a voice called to them, pulling Jon from his euphoric experience.

The boys whipped their heads around to see Terry Cummings jogging down the hall towards them. He took heavy breaths and beads of perspiration glistened on his forehead. The front of his shirt was plastered to his rounded belly, soaked in sweat. His green eyes were magnified behind the thick lenses of his glasses, and his almost-white blond hair bounced with every stride. He and his brother, Matt, lived in Bill and Chase's neighborhood. Terry was twelve. Matt was ten. They both looked the same, almost like twins but different ages.

"Hey," Jon said. "It's one half of the sperm brothers."

Bill and Chase snickered.

"Sperm brothers." Chase chuckled. "Ah, it never gets old."

Terry caught up with them, still huffing and puffing like he smoked three packs of Camels a day. "Thanks for waiting." Terry gave a few exhausted pants, bent over, and placed his hands on his knees.

"I'm surprised to see you," said Chase.

"Yeah, it's not every day someone fails PE," said Bill.

"Shut up. That's what I was doing," said Terry.

"What?" Jon asked.

"Coach Reeves said he wouldn't fail me if I ran for the entire period," Terry said. He stood erect and wiped his forehead with the back of his hand.

"Wow, lazy ass. Didn't think you had it in you." Jon patted Terry on the back. "Eww, gross." Sweat from Terry's shirt coated his fingers. He wiped them across Terry's cheek.

Terry twitched his head back. "Stop, you shit head." He pushed Jon's hand away. "My mom said if I failed PE, she wasn't gonna let me play video games or go to the movies at all this summer." Terry adjusted his backpack.

"Dammit," said Chase. "Guess we're stuck with you."

"Shut up, Dup," said Terry.

The boys exited the building and scurried down the steps. They stood outside, and Terry broke away from the group. "See y'all later. I gotta go find Matt."

"Later," Bill said.

Chase and Jon gave Terry a nod. The boys walked to the carpool line and waited for their rides.

2

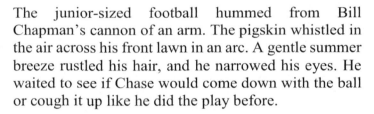

The junior-sized football hummed from Bill Chapman's cannon of an arm. The pigskin whistled in the air across his front lawn in an arc. A gentle summer breeze rustled his hair, and he narrowed his eyes. He waited to see if Chase would come down with the ball or cough it up like he did the play before.

It was the next evening, and the boys were in the middle of an intense game of football in the street of Bill Chapman's neighborhood. Bill, the most athletic of the three, always played quarterback. Chase and Jon took turns rotating on offense and defense, keeping score. It was a game the three twelve-year-olds had played since they were nine.

Jon led by one touchdown. He was the biggest of the three and tough as nails. His once pudgy body hit a growth spurt over the last year, and now with six extra inches, he had gotten leaner. His hair, which was usually spiked up on one side, lay flat as sweat dripped into his eyes. He waited for the ball to get close so he could knock the shit out of Chase.

And that's what happened.

Chase leaped up to catch the ball. Jon's feet left the ground, and he brought a shoulder into Chase's sternum. The blow proved too much for Chase's lanky body. He dropped the ball with an umph and crashed hard on the neighbor's front lawn two houses down. He landed flat on his back with his arms and legs sprawled, sputtering his lips.

Jon leaned over, staring at him with a smirk. "That's an incomplete pass. Fourth down, you scrawny shit."

Chase curled his hand from off the ground and gave Jon the bird. "Kiss my ass." He reached over and grabbed the football.

Jon threw his head back and cackled, "Number one on the field. That's me!" He gripped Chase's hand and helped him up.

"You hit like a vagina," Chase said, wiping the blades of the freshly cut grass off his body. He didn't wear a shirt, so the shavings stuck to his back like green stickers.

"You would know how vaginas hit," Jon fired back.

"Yeah, I hit your sister's last week." Chase made a thrusting motion with his hips.

Jon slapped him on the back of the head.

"Ouch," Chase winced.

"I don't have a sister, dumbass."

Chase went to respond but was interrupted by Bill's voice traveling across the yard.

"Dup, what the hell, man? That's two in a row." Bill held his arms outstretched, shaking his head.

Chase flipped Bill off. "Why don't you try taking a hit from Schwarzenegger here and see if you can hold on to the ball?"

"I thought you said I hit like a vagina." Jon raised an eyebrow.

"Shut up and get on offense so I can get you back." Chase shoved Jon on the shoulder, and the two boys jogged back to Bill's yard.

"Stop with the sissy excuses, soft serve, and toughen up," Bill yelled.

Chase flipped him the bird again.

"Is that all you know how to do?" Bill asked.

Chase jogged to Bill and tossed him the football. Bill caught it. The two boys stood face to face.

"No." Chase flipped him off with both hands.

"Genius, Dup. What a comeback." Bill scowled, unamused. He was sick of Chase dropping his perfect passes.

"Yeah, and I can do it in a variety of ways. Through the leg." Chase lifted his leg and stuck his arm under, flipping the bird. "Behind the back." He threw his arm around his back and gestured. "Under the arm and in your face." Chase lifted his fists, birds extended, and poked them in Bill's face.

Bill slapped Chase's hands away. "At least you can do something with your hands, 'cause Lord knows it isn't catching a football."

"Bill's right, Chase. You suck." Jon now joined his friends.

Chase glanced over his shoulder at Jon. "Don't make me kick your ass."

Jon snatched Chase by the back of the neck and tossed him to the ground. "Go home, stick boy."

Chase stumbled to all fours, snickering, then sat up in a kneeling position. "Almost there. My house is just down the road.' Chase pointed across the street.

Jon ignored his friend's smart-ass comment. He breathed in deep and exhaled, his mind wandering. He took in the aroma of a southern Louisiana evening— freshly cut grass and the smell of someone grilling next door. "Who's cooking?"

"Your mom," Chase said and stood up.

"Oh." Bill nodded towards the neighbor's. "Probably Mister LeBlanc. Been firing that grill up like clockwork every evening for the past week."

"What's he making?" Chase asked.

Bill shifted the football from arm to arm. "Asshole kids who ask stupid questions. How should I know?"

"Hey, Bill," Chase said.

"What?"

Chase held out his right fist, knuckles facing Bill. With his left hand, he made a cranking motion like he was reeling in a fish. He extended the middle finger of his left hand in a slow motion until it stood erect. "Fuck. You."

"Dup," Jon said. "Your lack of new material shows what an idiot you are."

"I agree." Bill threw the football at Chase, pegging him in the side of the leg. The slapping noise of leather meeting skin bellowed across the yard.

"Ouch. Shit. What was that for?" Chase's expression was riddled with confusion.

"Next time, I'll nail you in the nuts," said Bill.

Jon bent over in laughter. "Serves you right, Dup. I hope you break your middle fingers one day. Then what'll you do?"

Jon loved summer, but he loved Bill and Chase more. They had been his best friends for the past four years, inseparable since day one. He had a real soft spot in his heart for Chase. Underneath the smart-ass comments and mischievous grin lay a deep grave filled with hurt and fear. Chase's dad ran out on him, left when he was a young child. He'd had nothing to do with him or his mother over the years. For a while, Jon didn't think it bothered Chase. Until one night, while spending the night at Chase's house, Jon woke up to whimpers around three in the morning. Chase bawled his eyes out and spilled his guts to Jon about how much he missed his dad.

"Why does my dad hate me?" Chase had asked. "What did I do wrong? I feel like he can't stand me just because I exist."

Jon hugged his friend that night, embracing him hard. Whenever he thought about it, he could still feel Chase's tears in the nape of his neck. "Nothing," Jon had said. "You didn't do nothing wrong, Dup. But me and Bill, we love you. Our dads love you, too."

Ever since then, Chase gravitated towards Jon and Bill's dads as the male father figures in his life. They treated Chase as one of their own. The three boys were like brothers, and Jon wouldn't have it any other way.

A voice interrupted Jon's daydream.

"Hey, guys, can we play?"

It came from behind them.

The boys looked down the street to see Terry and Matt Cummings jogging towards them.

"Dammit, Terry," Jon said. "That's twice in two days you've interrupted my thoughts."

Terry shrugged and pushed his glasses up his nose.

"Derrrrr okay. It's the Cuuuuuuuu ah ah uh uh mmmming brothers!" Chase made a masturbating gesture with his hand and pretended to climax.

Bill and Jon never tired of the joke. They laughed and pointed at the brothers.

"Shut up, Dup," Terry said with a scowl.

"Yeah, shut up, Dup," Matt echoed.

"Is E.E. with you?" Jon asked. He glanced at Bill.

Bill chuckled, then had a coughing fit. "They're too stupid to even know who that is."

Terry flipped Jon off. "He's a poet, now fuck off."

"Oh yeah? What'd he write?" Chase asked.

"The book on assholes with your picture on the front." Terry flipped Chase off with his other hand, holding both middle fingers up at him.

"Wow, that's a popular gesture today," Jon said.

"Come on, y'all. Can we play?" Matt turned the toe of his shoe in the grass.

"Yeah, sure. Dup needs some more help getting his ass kicked," Bill said.

Chase nodded. "By all means," he said with a bow.

The five boys discussed how the teams would be divided. While they argued over who had to get stuck with Matt, a clattering sound rang out from across the street, followed by scraping noises. The boys stopped their chatter, and all five heads turned in the direction of the racket.

Three houses down on the left, where the road bent into a curve, an old man shuffled to his trash can. A navy-blue bathrobe hung off him like melting skin, and his red slippers swished across the driveway. He held a bottle of whiskey by the neck and kicked at a pile of VHS tapes scattered at his feet. He was a dirty, thin man with a gravel laden voice—unhealthy all over with a small beer gut. Veins like blue spider webs formed circular patterns across the top of his bald head, and the wispy, white hair on the side of his head flowed in the direction of the wind.

"Goddamn, motherfucking, cock-sucking fuck shits," he yelled in a raspy voice. He bent over to grab the tapes. Some whiskey splashed out of the bottle and onto the driveway. "Goddamn bottle! Stop fucking with me!"

He corralled the tapes and held them close to his chest. There were three total. The old man hobbled towards the trash, then paused. He felt the boys' eyes upon him and glared over at them. His expression morphed into a scowl, his lips and nostrils curling. The wrinkles in his face were as deep as canyons, and his yellow skin looked cigarette stained. His cheeks were flush, and wild blue eyes, which were set back deep in his head, told the boys to fuck off.

"Look, it's Old Man Mulligan," Chase said.

"His name's not Old Man Mulligan, dipstick," Terry said. He watched as the man stopped at the trash can. "It's Mad Man Max."

Jon grinned. "Whatever his name is, he's a creepy old bastard. And you live across the street from him, Bill."

Bill dropped his arms to his side and gripped the football in his hand. A somber mood came over all of them as the old man fiddled with the lid.

"His name's Edgar Craddock." Bill swallowed hard, his throat dry, partly from the heat and partly from having uttered that hair raising name. "He's lived there as long as I can remember. I don't go near him, much less talk to him. Legend has it, he used to be a looker back in the Stone Age."

"Pfff," Jon huffed. "Not even a cave woman would fuck limp dick over there."

The boys giggled, then Bill said, "No, for real. You know how popular the senior Rusty Babcock is?"

"Oh yes!" Terry clapped his hands together then placed them against his cheek. He tilted his head and fluttered his eyes. "We're all Madcock about Babcock."

Everyone laughed but Jon. "That fucker is a douche," he said.

"Beside the point." Bill said, still watching Edgar. "My mom told me stories about the old man. He was an athlete, and the girls loved him."

"Yeah, and my mom told me stories about Krampus so I wouldn't be such an ass around Christmas," Chase said. "Didn't work. Bullshit is bullshit is bullshit, Bill."

"I think we could refer to Bill's story as Bill shit." Jon put his arm around Bill.

Bill shrugged him off. "I'll Bill shit you, asshole. My mom doesn't lie."

"Oh, okay." Jon ignored Bill's shake off and put his arm back around him. He smirked and said, "Just like Chase over here doesn't have a millimeter peter."

"That's it, you turd!" Chase clenched his fists and went after Jon.

The mock fight was interrupted by the sound of glass clinking against concrete. The boys ceased their grab-assing and looked at the old man again.

Edgar Craddock had dropped his bottle of whisky, spilling it all over the driveway. "Fucking cock-sucking motherfucking ass wagon!" He lifted the lid off the trash can with a trembling hand and dumped the tapes, then slammed the lid shut and turned toward the boys. "What are you little sons a bitches looking at? Ain't you ever seen a man throw his shit out before?" Edgar's eyebrows danced up and down with the inflection of his voice. He bared his yellow teeth from across the street, spittle flying as he shook his fist.

"What's a matter? You a bunch a queers? Suck on it!" Edgar grabbed his crotch. When he finished with his insult, he leaned over and snatched the whiskey off the ground, tossing what little remained in his mouth. He let out a sigh, then said, "And, Bill Chapman, your mother's a whore!"

Chase and Jon responded with hearty belly laughs. Terry and Matt stood silent with mouths agape.

"Guess he was a lady's man," Chase said and cackled.

Bill ignored Chase and fired back at Craddock. "Hey, fuck you, old man!" Bill punched his fist in the air.

"Yeah, you'd like that, you little queer!" Edgar flipped him off, eyes not even giving Bill the time of day.

Jon and Chase went into a laughing fit. Terry and Matt looked as if they'd witnessed something they weren't supposed to, and Bill's entire face grew red.

Bill waved an arm. "Meh, the old fart ain't worth it. Nutcase."

"Yeah, Jon, you're right. He is a mean old

bastard," Chase said, giving a slow nod.

Edgar Craddock waddled to his front door.

"He's always busting our balls," Jon said.

Edgar arrived at his door and paused. He turned his head with a steady, creeping motion and gazed at Jon. His lightning blue eyes met Jon's deep hazel moons. Something forbidden yet familiar stirred in Jon's heart. It was like a buried secret arising after being underground for ages—a resurrected savior in the land of the forgotten. It was an imprint of the past, present, and future, merging into a timeless trinity.

Jon licked the white film of spit off his lips.

Edgar's eyes narrowed, and he raised the hand holding the whisky with his finger outstretched. He pointed at Jon and grinned.

Jon gave rapid blinks, then glanced down at the ground, breaking his gaze away from Craddock.

The old man laughed, opened the door, and went inside.

"I don't like him. There's something off with him." Terry sniffed and wiped his nose with the back of his hand.

"Oh, no shit, Sherlock, how'd you come to that conclusion?" Bill smacked Terry on the back of the head.

Terry winced. "Stop! No, I mean … he … he seems evil. Like, you know, the evil crazy dudes in the horror movies?"

Chase shook his head. "Nah, he's just a mean ole

curmudgeon."

The boys stood in a circle and stared at Edgar Craddock's house. The brown shutters had seen better days, and the once sun colored paint had now taken on a mustard tint.

Jon placed a hand on his hip. "What is his story, Bill?"

Bill tossed the football up in the air and caught it. "I already told you. All I know is he keeps to himself. I don't ever see anyone come to his house, or leave, for that matter. The only time I see him is when he comes out to get the mail or put something in the trash. He's always talking shit and saying mean things to everybody." Bill paused.

The boys studied their friend with anticipation, hanging on every word.

"Go on," Chase said.

Bill's eyes darted back and forth from his friends to the house, then stopped at Chase. "Last week, Mrs. Barbara's little five-year-old son, Josh, fell off his bike on the sidewalk there in front of Old Mad Man Max's house. Scraped his knees and chin up real good. The old fart was checking his mail. He hollered at the boy. 'You li'l piece a shit, stop your bellyaching and get your sissy ass the hell away from my house. You wanna cry? I'll make you cry. I'll cut your little balls off and feed them to my fish. When I'm done, I'll rip the flesh from your bones with my teeth and swallow it down while you watch! Now get!'"

"What a turd," Matt said.

"And you don't think he's evil?" Terry asked.

"He used to be a pharmacist," Bill continued. "Worked at the pharmacy right there off Hooper Road."

"What? That mean ole coot, a pharmacist?" Chase raised his eyebrows. "I'm surprised he never killed anyone. You know, give them the wrong meds on purpose or something like that?" He picked a piece of grass off his shoulder and flicked it to the ground.

"Yeah. That's all I know about him. I don't know if he has any family." Bill tossed the football up again and caught it.

The boys stood in silence for a moment, their gazes still glued on Edgar Craddock's house. Except for Bill. He kept tossing the ball up and catching it. He'd seen the house a million times, and it had lost its fascination. Matt watched as the wind banged a dangling eave near the corner of the house. Terry studied the big willow tree in the middle of the front yard and picked his nose. Chase caught a faint whiff of motor oil coming from under the carport. And Jon swatted at mosquitos buzzing around his head.

"What do you think is on those tapes?" Jon asked as he clapped his hands, killing a mosquito. A mischievous half-smirk crept across his face.

"Porn," Matt said and gave a shit-eating grin. Matt always said stupid stuff to try and be cool in front of everyone.

"You don't even know what that is!" Terry railed at him, his face scrunched in annoyance.

"I do too," Matt countered.

"No, you don't. You don't even know what sex is, so shut up and stop trying to be cool," said Terry.

"I bet it's evidence of him doing something. Something illegal," said Chase.

"And you think he'd just throw it in the trash where anyone could find it? Use your brain, moron." Bill was now interested in the conversation again. He looked at Jon. "What do you think's on there?"

Jon wasn't sure, but he wanted to find out. "I don't know, but we're gonna get those tapes."

"Ah, horseshit, Jon. It's probably old TBS movies and Dallas episodes," Chase snarled. He thought this whole damn thing was a waste of time. "Let's get back to playing."

"Hear me out for a minute." Jon broke away from the group and stood in front of them. He folded his hands, interlocking his fingers.

All the boys' eyes crept from the house to Jon, waiting for him to enlighten them.

"Bill, would you or would you not say that this creepy, sadistic old fart is the most mysterious dude you've ever laid eyes on?"

Bill bobbed his head in agreement.

Jon continued. "Right. What do we know about the old man?"

"We know he's lived here a hell of a long time and he used to be a pharmacist," Bill said.

"Yeah, and apparently used to be handsome and athletic," Chase added.

"Anything else?" Jon asked.

The boys paused for a moment in deep thought, then, one by one, shook their heads.

"Exactly," Jon said. "He could be a fugitive, or an outlaw. He could be hiding from the government. Even worse, he could be a Nazi!"

Matt gasped. The rest of the boys glanced at him like he still wet the bed.

Jon dismissed Matt's girly outburst. "All I'm saying is that we have a once-in-a-lifetime chance to gather more info on the mysterious Old Man Craddock." Jon held out his hands. "Guys, don't you see? Whatever is on those tapes could give us clues as to what the old cod is all about."

Bill made a fist, then jerked his elbow down to his side. "Yes! Oh, hell yeah, Jon! I hear you!"

"But who's gonna get the tapes?" Chase asked. He eased his head to the side in a slow, methodical motion, peeking around Jon's thoughtful gaze to Edgar's trash can.

All the boys' attention shifted there as well.

"Matt. Matt will go," Jon said, all matter of fact.

Matt twitched as if someone goosed him. "What? Me? I ain't going near Mad Man Max's house. Last time I got close, he threw canned goods at me. Hit me in the elbow, and it stayed swollen for, like, a week."

"That was, like, four years ago, pussy."

"So. Didn't you hear Bill's story about Josh? What if he catches me? He'll rape me with that whiskey bottle." Matt took a few steps back, mouth open like a fish.

"Matt, you idiot, you don't even know what that means. Stop being a sissy and go get the tapes," Terry said and closed the distance on his brother.

"Well, Terry. If you're such a badass, why don't you go get them?" Matt stood his ground.

"You're all nothing but a truck load of vaginas. I'll go get the damn tapes." Jon spat on the ground, disgusted. His eyes narrowed as he glared at Matt. "Dammit, Matt, I was trying to stick up for you. Give you a chance to show you're not the little soft serve we all thought you were. Guess you are a wuss." Jon spun around to march to the trash can when a hand gripped his shoulder.

"No, I'll go," Matt said and squeezed Jon's shoulder. "But I think we should wait till it gets dark. Mad Man Max will be shitfaced then and won't notice a thing."

Jon turned to Matt and slapped him on the back. "That a boy. I knew you had it in you. And yeah, good idea." Jon's attention shifted to Bill, who traced his hands across the football. "Bill, what time is it?"

Bill took his hand off the football and brought his black Casio wristwatch into view. "Seven forty-five."

Jon gazed up at the sky. "We got about thirty minutes or so till sunset. Bill, set your alarm for eight thirty. It'll be dark for sure. Plus, it gives Old Man

Craddock another forty-five minutes to suck on that bottle."

There were some beeping noises, then Bill said, "All set."

"Come on. Let's go wait on Bill's porch," Chase said. He led the way, and the rest of the gang followed.

As Jon strolled along the grass, he thought about how proud he was of Matt for doing this. Though Jon gave Matt and Terry shit, he loved them to death. The two brothers started going to the same school as Bill, Chase, and Jon that past year. They came from a broken home and lived with their mother in Bill and Chase's neighborhood. Their dad was around every once in a while, but not enough to be called an "involved" father. To make matters even worse, when the brothers started school, they were bullied every day.

Shane Hebert was a year older than Terry, Bill, Jon, and Chase but was a grade below them because he had failed twice. One day in the bathroom, Shane pissed in a thermos and, while Terry was taking a shit, dumped it over the stall. Terry was covered from head to toe in urine. The next day, Shane went after Matt as well. He held him down on the ground and shoved chalk up his nose.

Matt and Terry wished they had a dad to go to and talk to about it. They wished they had a pops who would have stood up for them or told them how to handle the situation. Instead, they had Jon, Bill, and Chase.

Jon found out about the bullying, then talked to

Bill and Chase. The boys knew where Shane lived, and they also knew his parents didn't get home from work until after six. The following day after school, they bought a bunch of chalk and dumped it in a pillowcase. They got on their bikes and rode two miles down the road to Shane's house.

Shane answered the door, and the boys barged in on him. Shane staggered backwards. Bill and Chase yanked on his hair and arms until they could get him secure. As they held him, Jon twirled the pillowcase of chalk tight. He cocked his arms back and swung it like a baseball bat. There was a loud smack and a crunching sound as the chalk busted on Shane's face.

Bill and Chase let go while Jon beat the shit out of Shane with the pillowcase until all the chalk was shattered. Shane had lain on the ground crying and spitting out blood. Bill, Chase, and Jon unzipped their flies, then urinated on Shane.

"You ever even look at Terry and Matt again," Jon had said, "so help me God, I will put rocks in the pillowcase next time."

No one bullied Matt or Terry again.

Once the boys arrived at Bill's porch, they sat and discussed the things most twelve-year-old males talk about—girls, sports, and wrestling.

"I still can't get over the fact that Hulk Hogan lost to the Ultimate Warrior in WrestleMania," Jon said as he rocked in the chair.

"Yeah, me too," Bill said. He rocked away in the

chair next to Jon.

Chase sat on the ground beside Jon, watching as moths fluttered around the light. He glanced at Jon, then said, "And none of us will forget Jon's little temper tantrum on that memorable day back in April."

"Shut up, Dup." Jon kicked at Chase.

"Why, what happened?" Matt asked. He sat on the ground against the railing and faced Jon and Bill.

Terry stood and leaned on the railing, taking an interest in the story.

"Let me relay the events of that most memorable evening," Chase said and held up his pointer finger. "After sitting there stunned for a few minutes, Jon leaped up from the couch and threw the pillows and said, 'This is bullshit!' Then he stormed up the steps to his room."

"Damn," Matt said.

"I can so see Jon doing that," Terry said and snickered.

Jon rocked and smiled, waiting for Chase to continue the story.

"Then," Chase said, "we followed Jon up to his room. When we walked in, there was pissed-off Jon tearing his Hogan poster off the wall and ripping it to shreds." Chase made thrashing noises and did the motions with his hands. "He was yelling, 'You are supposed to kick out of their finisher moves, dammit! And largest arms in the world? Twenty-four-inch pythons? Horseshit!' Man, look. We couldn't believe Hulk lost either. Jon's the biggest Hulk Hogan fan we ever knew. We had a feeling he'd be upset if he lost." Chase paused. "But not like this."

"A little over dramatic, don't you think, Jon?" Terry leaned up from the railing. "I mean, it's all fake."

"Oh shit, here we go," Bill said, rolling his eyes.

Chase hung his head. "Oh, Lord. No he didn't."

"What?" Terry held out his arms. "What did I say?"

Jon eased up from the chair, and Chase scurried to his feet.

"Dup," Jon said, crossing his arms.

"It's that time, isn't it?" Chase hung an arm around Jon's neck.

"Terry, follow me out to the yard." Jon uncrossed his arms and removed Chase's hand from around him. He walked by Terry and shoulder bumped him.

Terry huffed, bobbled back a step, and caught himself on the railing.

Chase stopped to talk to Terry. "Demonstration time, asshole. You think it's fake? Step right this way." Chase held out his arms.

"Oh God, I love it when Jon does this," Bill said. He jumped up from the chair and ran into the front yard.

Matt got up and jogged over to his brother. He placed his hands on his shoulders and said, "Been nice knowing you." He gave Terry a pat and moseyed to the front yard.

Terry's heart sank. He didn't know what was about to happen, but he was nervous as hell. His palms were sweaty, and his testicles tried to crawl inside his stomach.

"Hey, blind and blond, get out here," Jon yelled.

Terry swallowed hard. He breathed in deep and exhaled. "Dammit, I'm coming!" But he didn't want to go. He knew whatever was about to happen wasn't going to be pleasant.

"Of course you are," Bill yelled and made a masturbation gesture with his hand. "Cause you're a cuuuuu … ahhhh … uuuuumings brother!"

"Front and center." Jon pointed at the ground.

Terry took nervous steps over to Jon. The blades of grass giving way under his feet seemed to echo like crunching ice in his ears. He had never been on the bad side of Jon before. He had the urge to shit his pants and run away. But he didn't. If he even tried to get out of this, he would for certain take Matt's place as the resident "pussy."

Terry stood face to face with Jon. He licked his lips and ran a hand through his hair. "Listen, Jon—"

"Shut up," Jon said.

Terry glanced to his right, then left. Bill, Chase, and Matt all snickered and pointed at him.

"Dup?" Jon asked.

"Yes?" Chase responded. He clasped his hand over his mouth and chuckled. He knew what came next.

"What is one of the most basic wrestling moves?"

"Hmmmmm," Chase said and rubbed his chin. "I don't know." He held out his hands. "A body slam, maybe?"

"Yes," Jon said and gave a thumbs up. "A body slam."

"Whoa, wait!" Terry raised his hands in protest and took a step back. "No way!"

"It's fake, remember." Jon eased towards Terry.

"No, Jon!" Terry whipped his body around in the opposite direction and tried to run away. Tough guy cover blown. His pussiness was on full display.

Jon grabbed him by the back of the hair.

"Ouch! Son of a bitch, Jon," Terry yelled.

Jon pulled Terry back and spun him around. He placed an arm around his shoulder and slipped another between his thighs. Jon hoisted Terry up and tilted his body towards the ground.

"Stop! Stop! Stop!" Terry shrieked.

Bill, Chase, and Matt doubled over in hysterics

"How is this for fake?" Jon slammed Terry on the ground of Bill's front lawn.

Terry landed with a hefty thump, the breath puffing out of him. He didn't make any more sounds for a few moments. He just arched his body, placing his hand on his lower back. His mouth was open, and his eyes clenched shut in pain. Sweat beaded down his forehead, and his glasses sat cockeyed on his face.

"How fake is it now, dipshit?" Jon spat on the

ground.

Terry gave a few rapid breaths, then said. "That fucking hurt, you bastard."

Jon walked over to Terry and leered down at him. "Of course it did. Tell me wrestling is fake again, and I will put you in a sleeper hold."

"Dammit. Okay, okay," Terry said in submission.

Jon held out a hand. Terry obliged, and Jon hoisted him off the ground.

"Summer Slam is coming up soon," Jon said and let go of Terry's hand. "Hogan is facing Earthquake, and The Hart Foundation takes on Demolition for the tag team championship. Want to come watch with us?"

Terry centered his glasses and wiped the grass off his arms. "Yeah," he said, nodding. "Sure."

"Sure as shit." Jon ruffled Terry's hair.

"Hey." Terry pulled back and swatted Jon's hand away. "Yeah. Sure as shit,' he said.

"Dup! Bill!" Jon's eyes shifted to his friends.

"What?" Bill asked.

"We got one more for Summer Slam." Jon eyed Matt. "You wanna come?"

"Hell yeah," Matt said.

"Sounds good to me," Bill said.

Jon and Terry locked eyes again. Terry smiled back at Jon with relief. He was in the pack now, and Jon would have his back through thick and thin.

"Good," Jon said. "Let's go back to the porch and wait for our chance with Mad Man Max."

Jon headed back to his rocking chair, and the boys followed. This summer was going to be one of the best of Jon's life; he could sense it. With the change in his appearance, the girls took notice. He thought about Laurianne kissing his cheek yesterday and it made his heart happy. Jon had called her that same evening and invited her over to his house for next weekend to hang out and watch movies. He also had asked her to shoot firecrackers with him and the guys on the 4th of July before she went out of town to Florida. She agreed to that as well. But Jon had more than shooting firecrackers on his mind for those nights. He planned on making the move and landing his first real kiss. The French kind; the one with tongue.

3

———————|———————

Jon gripped the arms of the rocking chair and sat back down. Bill scootched his rocker a tad closer to Jon and nestled in. There was a post in the middle of the porch with the center rotting out. Terry marked his territory there, lowering his haunches and making himself at home. Matt and Chase stood at respective ends of the opening where the walkway ran into the porch. They each rested an arm on the wooden poles next to them.

The front door of the porch opened with a grating squeak. Cory Chapman, Bill's older brother, who was going to be a junior at Central High, stuck his head out. "What are you bunch of maxi pads doing?"

Jon arched his head back in the chair and looked at Cory. "Would've been your girlfriend, but she's too sore from last time."

"Hahaha," Bill laughed. "He got you there, you sphincter!"

Cory slid his body out the door, swatting with his

arm at Jon. "Jon Benson, you've never even had a boner."

"That's not what your mom said." Jon jerked his head out of the way.

"Ah, sick, dude!" Bill backhanded Jon across the chest. "She's my mom, too. What the fuck?"

Cory stepped behind Jon and smacked him on top of the head. "Yeah, dumbass." Cory stood about five feet ten inches tall. He styled his long, black hair in a ponytail with a blue bandana wrapped around the top of his head. Today he wore an Iron Maiden T-shirt, with a cigarette pack rolled up in his left sleeve, and a pair of denim jeans. He drove a blue Camaro and carried a knife. He also smoked a pack a day and kept a condom in his wallet. Bill and his friends thought his brother was a badass.

"Hey, Cory." Chase gave him a head nod.

"Dup," Cory said and stopped messing with Jon. "You still wetting the bed?"

"Fuck you," Chase said, flipping the bird.

"That's today's favorite gesture," Bill said.

"Yeah, the only one Dup seems to know," Jon said.

Chase took both hands and waved them at Bill and Jon. He flipped the bird with each one, turning them so the tips of his middle fingers faced them. He made a machine gun noise with his mouth and moved his hands back and forth.

"See," Jon said.

Cory ignored Chase. "For real, Bill. What are y'all

doing?"

Bill's shoulder's rose and fell. "Nothing. Just sitting here."

Cory's eyes searched the boys. They didn't look guilty. Not yet, anyway. "Bullshit," Cory said. He unrolled his pack of cigarettes from his sleeve and pulled a matchbook from his pocket. He slipped out a cig and lit up. "You fuckers are up to something." Cory puffed and exhaled.

"No," Jon said. "Just trying to recover from an encounter with Mad Man Max."

The pupils in Cory's dark blue eyes dilated and his eyelids slanted. He took another drag off his cigarette. "Edgar Fucking Craddock. God, what a fucked-up individual."

"What do you know about him?" Chase asked.

"Enough to know to stay away," Cory said.

Bill snapped his head around. "What? You never told me you knew anything about Craddock."

Cory narrowed his eyes at Bill. "Drop it."

"You dick!" Bill was turned halfway around in the rocker. "You do know something?"

Cory put the cigarette to his lips and inhaled. "I said, drop it." The smoke exited his mouth and nostrils as wispy clouds.

"Oh, come on, Cory," Jon said. "You can't leave us hanging."

Cory took a long drag and exhaled. "What did he

do to y'all?"

"Nothing," Chase said. "Just came out to his trash can to throw stuff away. Saw us and started talking shit."

The other boys glared at Chase, their looks telling him he better not say a damn word about the tapes.

"What was he throwing away?" Cory asked.

Chase didn't give away the secret. "Nothing. Hell, I don't know. Just a trash bag."

"Yeah." Cory bent over and snubbed the end of his cigarette out on the concrete.

"You gonna tell us what you saw?" Jon asked.

Cory gave Craddock's house a long stare. "Stay away from that house. Don't even go near it."

"Why?" Bill asked.

Cory eased out from behind Jon's chair and stood next to Bill. He leered down at him. "You wanna know? You really wanna know?"

Bill looked up at his brother and gave a slow nod.

"All right, limp dicks. I'll tell ya. First, get outta my seat." Cory grabbed Bill by the collar and yanked.

"Hey! Fuckwad," Bill yelled. He tried to fight Cory off, but he was too strong. At five inches taller and four years older, Bill didn't have a prayer. "Fine! I'll get up. Just get off me!"

Cory let go of Bill and took his seat in the chair. He gazed out at the heap of shit Craddock called a home and rocked. "It was around the time I quit baseball. Freshman year."

Bill's mouth gaped like a koi fish. Cory never talked about freshman year. Never. If one were to look at Cory today, they would never assume he used to be the golden boy all-star athlete. But something happened freshman year. Something he never told Bill nor their parents about. It was something so damaging, Cory quit baseball, ditched all his athlete friends, and started hanging out with the metal heads. His current girlfriend, Lacy, was a blonde-haired, blue-eyed goth chic who was big into Wicca and Witchcraft. That was another major change in Cory. He went from being sort of a religious agnostic who went to church on Sundays because his parents made him to being immersed in the occult. The therapist said there was nothing to worry about. This was normal teenage rebellion and nothing was wrong with Cory. Bill never believed it. Not for one second. Who goes from being an all-star left-handed pitcher to a recluse metal head without some major shit going down?

"It was a dare," Cory continued. "Sort of an initiation to the varsity team. See, I was good enough to skip junior varsity. Coach wanted me ready to be on the mound freshman season, so I got broken in good. The stories about Mad Man Max have been going around for a long time. Everyone knew I lived across the street from him. I mean, how could they not. The fucker is sort of a psychotic legend around here."

"Yeah, no shit," Chase said.

"For my initiation, I had to be locked in the old man's house for two hours. If I got scared or asked to come out, they were gonna shave my head and all my pubic hairs."

"Remind me never to play sports," Terry said.

"You suck too bad anyway," Chase said. "You'd never make the team."

"Fuck you, Dup," Terry shot back.

"Hey, assholes," Cory yelled. "You gonna let me finish?"

Chase held out his hand, motioning for Cory to proceed.

"Anyway, one weekend, Old Man Craddock was gone. He used to drive an old electric-blue El Camino. Real piece of shit, with the bumper sagging and everything. You could hear it before you could see it. Bobby, Kyle, and Randy were over. They were juniors. Sent to make sure I did what I was supposed to do or else. It was around dusk, so as soon as the sun went down, we snuck over to Craddock's." Cory stopped talking, took a drag, and rocked. His facial muscles tensed, and he dug his fingernails into the arms of the rocker. He exhaled the smoke, and it whirled around his face like early morning fog.

"What happened next?" Jon asked.

Cory glanced up at Jon, then back at the house. "That damn car has been up on those blocks and under that tarp for God knows how long."

The boys looked at the blue Trans Am under the tarp, the wind blowing up the corners, revealing parts of the rear end.

Cory continued. "The back door to the house was

open. I mean, cracked open, you know? Not even shut all the way. Bobby, Randy, and Kyle handed me a flashlight and said to get at it. I was a little nervous, you know? But I tried to play it cool. I snatched the light from them and went in. The guys went back across the street and waited on the porch.

"It was dark. No lights on. I turned on my flashlight and checked out the kitchen. It was fucking disgusting, man. There were open tuna cans that had been there for God knows how long. There was a big-ass slab of rotting meat just sitting on the counter. Full of fucking maggots. There were all kinds of stains everywhere. All over the counter and walls. All over the floor. It was a mess."

"That's so gross," Bill said, shuddering.

"Smelled even worse," Cory said. "But that's not the fucked-up part. Not even by far, man."

The boys traded uneasy glances.

Cory took another long drag, burning the cigarette to the butt. He breathed out and flicked the end into the yard. "I turned and shined the light on the kitchen table."

Cory snatched the pack of Camels off his lap and lit up again. He smoked and rocked, not saying a word. He just stared across the street at Craddock's house. The look in his eyes was guarded, as if some forbidden knowledge lay locked away inside them. He debated internally about whether or not he would continue the story. What would be gained if he did? Nothing. But what if he didn't? What if Bill and his dumbass friends were thinking of going over there and trying to get

Craddock back? Yeah, he had to warn them. Cory decided to tell them everything.

"The kitchen table was covered with a black cloth and candles and shit. And I swear to God it looked like human body parts scattered all across it."

"What?" Matt squealed.

"No fucking way," Bill said.

"Yes fucking way," Cory said.

"What did you do?" Jon asked.

"I just stood there. Staring at the carnage. Some of the body parts were so mangled it looked like hamburger meat. Fingers, toes, legs … and a penis, I think. A penis and part of a tit."

"Oh God, I think I'm gonna be sick." Terry turned his head to the side and took deep breaths.

"I was in shock," Cory said. "Couldn't believe what I was seeing. I don't know how long I had been staring there, but the sound of Craddock's car turning in the driveway and the lights through the window snapped me out of it. I turned off my flashlight and dropped to all fours. I started to crawl towards the back door when I heard footsteps approach. I did the only thing I could do at that moment. I crawled under the table and hid behind some of the chairs that were tucked in."

"Jesus Christ, Cory," Bill said. "How did you get out?"

"I could see right into the living room from where I was at. Craddock walked the girl over to the couch. I got a good glimpse of her. She wasn't a looker, that's for sure. She looked strung out on meth. Dressed in a pink sundress a few sizes too big. Looked like it was about to fall off of her. Craddock walked over to the wall and flipped a switch. And this is when things got really fucked." Cory brought the cigarette to his lips. He hit it a few more times before he continued.

"The walls, man. The fucking walls. This massive symbol just lit up on the back wall."

"What kind of symbol?" Jon asked.

Cory shook his head. "I don't know. Like nothing I had ever seen. Even now, I can't find anything like it in the occult. It was a circle with triangle shapes in it, the corners busting out the sides of the circle. Also had some other lines through it. The best I can describe it is that it looked like some offshoot of a pentagram. But there it was, shining on the wall in this bright neon red color."

"Holy fuck," Chase said.

"Yeah," Cory agreed. "Then, he bent that girl over and started banging her from behind. Where I was at, I could see her from the front. Hands on her thighs and hair dangling in her face. That pink dress sagged almost down to the floor, and I could see her nasty tits flopping back and forth."

"Oh God." Terry got grossed out again.

"You could hear their nasty skin smacking against each other. Over and over, like a splatting sound. Splat, splat, splat, splat. The most god-awful sound ever. Then the girl started screaming. And I'm not talking about yelling. I'm talking about screaming like she was in the worst pain of her life."

"What was Craddock doing to her?" Chase asked.

"I don't know if it was Craddock. I don't know what it was. Next thing I see is her skin starts to melt off in gobs. It started with her face. Chunks of it just started sliding off and plopping onto the floor. Her cheeks, then lips, then her nose fell off. After that, she gagged and coughed and spit her tongue across the room. It landed a few feet on the floor in front of the table where I was at. I got a good look at it. It still wiggled a bit, you know, shaking back and forth. Almost like a snake when it gets its head cut off. Her eyes popped out next. And, oh God!" Cory's eyes watered. He looked down at his cigarette with a disgruntled look, then flicked it into the yard.

"Cory, it's okay if—"

Cory cut Bill off. "Her eyes just dangled there. From her head, the sockets spewed all kinds of fluid. Craddock still pounded away behind her, made her eyes spin in circles as they hung there. He then tore her dress off. Violently. Just ripped it right off her. The skin all over her body started to fall off. Her tits, man. They just slid off and dripped to the floor in two big globs. Then all the rest of her skin just oozed off her. There was this massive splattering sound as her stomach opened up and her guts just sloshed to the ground. All the while, Craddock just fucked away, laughing."

"I don't think I want to hear anymore," Terry said.

"Well too fucking bad," Cory snarled. "It ain't

over. Not by a long shot. This lady, you see, she started to change. As her skin melted off, there was something underneath her. Some thing. Horns grew out of the eye sockets. The thing's skin was black and leathery. Bulging muscles, long, black fingernails. It was a thing of nightmares. And I guess Craddock finished shooting his wad because the goddamn thing stood up, flung off the remaining skin, and then followed Craddock back to the bedroom. That's when I got the fuck out of there."

The boys sat in uncomfortable silence, letting Cory's words hang in the air for an eternity. Terry had scooched his knees up to his chest and buried his face in them. Jon, Bill, and Chase didn't say a word. Blank stares adorned their faces, and they blinked their eyes. Matt stood with his hands in his pockets, watching an ant scurry along the driveway.

"You don't walk away from something like that unchanged," Cory said. "So, now you five fuckbags know what happened. And listen to me when I tell you." Cory bolted up in the rocker. His eyes examined each boy. "Stay the hell away from that house. Do you hear me? Just leave the old man alone."

None of them looked Cory in the eyes. They weren't sure if he was telling the truth or if this was a bullshit story to try and get under their skin.

Cory got up from the chair. "I gotta go. Going to meet Lacy and smoke some weed and listen to music." He ruffled Bill's hair. "Y'all have fun, and don't do anything stupid." He opened the door and went inside.

Bill plopped back down in the rocker and kicked

his feet up on the porch rail. "Holy shit, that was intense."

"I didn't know your brother was that messed up," Chase said. "I mean, I knew he had issues, but damn."

"Yeah, I almost puked, like, two times," Terry said.

"That's because you're a pussy," Chase said.

"Fuck off," Terry said, jutting his chin at Chase.

"Yeah, well, I think he's full of shit," Matt said.

Jon's eyes slanted, and his eyebrows raised to a point. "Is he?"

"Oh, he is definitely full of shit," Chase said.

"I don't know." Bill dropped his feet to the ground and sat up. "I've never seen him like that before."

The plan to get the tapes was in jeopardy. The stakes were now a hell of a lot higher. What if Cory was telling the truth? If Craddock caught them, he'd kill them for sure. And if not, then Cory pulled a hell of a fast one on them and made them all look like a bunch of vaginas. Uncertainty exuded from all their faces. All of them except Jon.

"He's telling the truth," Jon said.

"What makes you so sure?" Chase asked.

"Like Bill said. I've known Cory longer than any of you. Never seen him that shaken up before."

"Well, if he is telling the truth, no way am I going near that house to get those fucking tapes," Matt said.

Jon jolted up in his chair. "The hell you aren't!"

"Jon, you can't be serious?" Terry asked. He scratched his head and glared at Jon like he'd left his brain back in the yard. "After what Cory just told us? If there is any truth whatsoever in what he said, we need to stay away."

"No," Jon shot back. "If what he said was true, we need to get those tapes. We've been through this. There might be evidence on those tapes. Don't you see? What Cory told us just confirms we need to get them."

"I hate to say this," Bill said, "but I agree with Jon." He stood up, placed his arms on the railing, and gave a solemn stare at Craddock's house. "What my brother saw fucked him up. Fucked him up good. I'm gonna make that bastard pay! Do you hear me!?" Bill balled his hand into a fist and struck the railing. "Do you hear me!? That fucker has to pay. We are getting those tapes, goddamnit! And, Matt, if you are too chicken shit to do it, I will!"

Matt turned his toe on the walkway, smashing the ant he'd been watching earlier. "I'll go," he mumbled.

"Matt, come on!" Terry held out his arms, pleading with his brother.

"It's okay. I … I want to do it." And Matt did. This wasn't about him anymore. Seeing how bad Cory had been fucked up by what he saw in there made Matt want to right the wrongs. Bill was his friend too, and he wanted to do this for him. He also wanted to get the guys off his back. He never let on, but being called a "puss" all the time got to him. This would ensure his place among the group as brave like Jon. A boy who faced his fear and pissed all over it.

"Fine," Terry said. "It's your funeral, you stupid shit." He looked at Jon. "You aren't gonna let him do this, are you?"

Jon curled his lips downward. "Not my decision. He said he wants to do it."

"Yeah, okay." Terry crossed his arms. "So what are we gonna do now?"

"We wait," Jon said. "And then we move forward as planned."

4

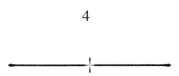

While they waited on the porch, Bill and Chase argued over whether David Justice or Frank Thomas was the best rookie of the season. Terry and Jon talked more about wrestling, and Matt listened in on both conversations, paying more attention to the one about wrestling. He had heard Bill and Chase argue so many times over Justice and Thomas, it was nauseating.

The mood had lightened a bit, then Bill's watch beeped. Dread settled over the boys again like an ominous storm cloud.

Terry, who sat next to his brother, tapped Matt on the shoe and tried to lighten the mood again. "All right, Maverick, time to enter the Danger Zone." It was a failed attempt.

The boys stood up and dusted off their bottoms. The sun had set, and it was now dark outside, casting summertime shadows across the neighborhood.

Jon thought about Cory's story and about Matt

getting the tapes. A brilliant idea came to his mind. "Hey, Matt, come here."

Matt shuffled over to the center of the porch next to Jon. "What?"

Jon gave a wink to the guys, then turned his attention to Matt. "We're all proud of you for stepping up like a man and doing this."

Jon's confidence and playful spirit put the boys at ease. The boys nodded, and Matt pushed up his glasses.

The bug zapper hanging in the back corner of the porch went off.

"Gah!" Matt flinched, covering his head with his arms.

"Oh, God," Bill laughed. "He got spooked by the bug zapper, Jon."

"Yeah," Chase agreed. "How the hell is he gonna get within fifty feet from Mad Man Max's?"

"Matt," Terry pleaded. "Come on, you don't have to do this." He knew the look in his brother's eyes. The "I am scared shitless and three seconds away from pissing myself" look.

Jon held his hand up, motioning for the chatter to stop. "There's one more thing I want you to do," he said to Matt. "If you do this, I swear we won't call you sissy, pussy, wussy, wimp, soft serve, pudding pop, Jello hole, or no nuts anymore."

"You left out Casper the Castrated Ghost and NoBroCock," Chase said.

"Wait a minute," Bill protested. "That's a big

bargain. I ain't promising nothing till I hear what you got in mind there, Jon."

"Fair enough," Jon agreed. "After Matt grabs the tapes, I want him to take a peek in Craddock's window."

Gasping, ohs and ahs filled the air.

Matt's face turned pale and he clinched his butt cheeks. The concept of being so scared you shat your pants almost became a reality for Matt.

"I'll agree to stop calling him all the names previously listed if he does that," Chase said.

Jon raised an eyebrow at Bill and Terry. They agreed, with reluctance, so Jon continued.

"This is huge, Matt. We know nothing about the old man. Getting a glimpse of the inside of his house might confirm whether or not Cory was telling the truth. What do you say? Will you take a peek?"

Silence from Matt. The frogs croaked, the crickets sang, and Matt swallowed so hard it sounded as if he tried to get down a golf ball. Look in the window? After what happened to Cory? True or not, it freaked Matt the fuck out. What the hell was Jon trying to do, kill him?

Everything in Matt screamed at him to walk away. Let them call him NoBroCock or Casper the Castrated Ghost. It didn't matter, and it sure as hell wasn't as scary as Mad Man Max's house.

"Yeah," Matt said. For some goddamn stupid reason, he agreed to it.

"Good," Jon said. He removed his arm from around Matt's neck, then slapped him hard on the ass.

Matt winced and furrowed his brow at Jon. "Hey," he protested.

"Now get the fuck over there and get the damn tapes," Jon said. "And, Bill? Turn off the porch light."

Bill flipped the switch and turned out the light. Matt adjusted his shirt collar, took a deep breath, and exhaled. He could smell the faint stench of the Chapmans' trash as the summer breeze carried it to his nose.

Craddock's house hid in the shadows of the Louisiana night. There were secrets behind those walls, and Matt knew it—secrets no young boys should look into, much less uncover. A den of debauchery and abominations. A cesspool of sinfulness and sacrilege. A place in which once you see the inside, you will never see the light of day again.

Edgar Craddock.

A mean old bastard.

A man of mystery.

The enigma of the neighborhood.

And Matt was about to bring it all into the light.

Matt found strength, and his shaky legs carried him down the concrete steps of the porch and out into the yard. He no longer had the urge to shit himself, so he relaxed his body. Droplets of perspiration dripped down his face, glimmering in the moonlight. Matt trekked through Bill's yard and onto the sidewalk. He stopped under a streetlight, then turned his torso halfway to give his friends one last look.

The scene reminded Jon of the cover of The Exorcist—the one with Father Merrin arriving outside of Ragan's home and standing under the streetlamp. He had never watched the movie or read the book, but he had held the tape in his hands many times at the video store, trying to work up the courage to rent it. An eerie tingle made its way up Jon's spine, as if a million ants marched all the way to his brain. He didn't think it was such a good idea for Matt to go alone.

"The Exorcist," Jon whispered.

"What?" Bill's face soured.

Jon, gaze still fixed on Matt standing frozen under the streetlight, said it louder this time, pointing. "The Exorcist, man. The cover? Father Merrin standing under the streetlamp?"

"Oh shit, man, you're right," Chase said.

Jon interpreted it as a bad omen. "I'm not letting him go alone." He broke away from the group and jogged toward Matt.

"What the hell?" Bill didn't understand what all the fuss was about. "Jon has lost his shit," Bill said, staring at Chase.

"I didn't see you volunteering to go to the house," Chase said.

"Shut up, asswipe. And I did, too." Bill pushed Chase on the shoulder.

"Stop, you two. You're ruining the show," Terry

said.

Chase flipped Bill off. "Yeah, you're ruining the show."

"I'll kick your ass later," Bill said, turning his attention back to Jon and Matt.

"Matt. Matt, wait up," Jon called in a whisper yell. His sneakers skidded on the sidewalk, and he came to a halt.

Matt's face was a concoction of confusion and relief. "What are you doing?"

"I don't know." Jon shrugged. "I'm a sucker for these sort of spooky things. I didn't want you having all the fun."

Matt smirked. "Cool."

Jon put an arm around Matt. "Yeah, cool. Let's go."

The two boys stepped off the sidewalk and onto the street. They tip-toed like graceful ballerinas to Edgar Craddock's driveway. They paused, standing stoic as statues, and stared down the dimly lit driveway. Jon removed his arm from around Matt.

The concrete sprouted grass and weeds between its cracks, making the cement resemble stepping stones rather than a driveway. A dilapidated blue Trans-Am sat on cinder blocks under the carport, and a red Snapper riding lawn mower was next to it, covered half way with a blue tarp. To the right, against the wall, was an old bookshelf decorated with mason jars filled with God knew what along with what looked like old books and magazines. The rest of the house looked beat to hell. The wood was rotten in places, and the lawn looked like it hadn't been cut in months.

"What a shithole," Matt mumbled, his face wrinkling behind his glasses.

"Never mind the décor. Grab the tapes." Jon motioned at the trash can with his head.

Matt looked to his right. The tin trash can was about ten feet from them. It was dented on one side and speckled with rust. The lid sat askew, not fitting tight because of the warped shape of the can. Jon walked over, grabbed the handle to the lid, and removed it. The smell hit them like a punch in the gut. Jon put his face in the crook of his arm, and Matt made a weird half-snort, half-hacking sound.

"Oh man, that's rank," Matt whispered.

"Smells like rotten meat and turds." Jon pulled his head out of his arms and approached the can.

The three tapes sat on top. Next to them, partly covered by torn pages from a magazine, was a black knife and a soiled adult diaper. Jon wanted to puke, but he couldn't help but giggle at the sight of the diaper.

"Matt, come look. Ole Mister Craddock, I mean Crappock." Jon made a quick motion with his hand.

Matt joined Jon at the trash can and looked in. He slapped his hands over his face, both to hide himself from the smell and keep the chuckles at bay. "Dude, that smells so bad."

"Yeah, like old people and rotting potted meat."

Jon lifted his eyes and gazed out over the dark

landscape toward Bill's house.

Terry, Chase, and Bill stood on pins and needles, wondering what the hell was going on and what the hell could be so funny. Bill held his arms up.

Jon reached down and grabbed the knife handle. It was a carving knife and the blade had been thrust through the diaper. Jon raised the diaper out of the can for the other boys to see. As he did, the diaper fell open. A waterfall of maggots flowed from the exposed inside, as did severed, rotting tongues. Jon and Matt didn't recognize the tongues for what they were, but there was no mistaking the rest.

"Ah, sick! What the hell?" Matt leaped back as if the trash can had exploded.

"Nasty-ass old fart." Jon, unmoved, flung the diaper off the blade and into the trash.

Laughter broke out across the street.

Jon scowled and placed a finger over his lip. "Shhh, quiet you bunch of retards." Jon knew they couldn't hear him, but there was no way in hell he was going to let his voice rise above a whisper. He lifted the knife up into the moonlight. Dried blood was caked across the lower half of the blade.

"Jon?" Matt stared into the trash can. "Were those maggots?"

"Yes."

"What were those rotten looking things that fell out of the diaper?"

"Probably rotten pieces of sausage."

"You sure?"

"Yes, dammit. Now grab the tapes before we get found out." Jon tossed the knife into the trash can.

Matt squinched his eyes shut and turned his head. He reached down into the trash can. "Open your eyes, dumbass, and stop being a bitch," Jon scolded.

Matt slid his hands into something warm and mushy. His eyes popped open and his head

whipped in the direction of the can. "Fucking disgusting!" His hands rose from the abyss of the can. "Oh my God," Matt said as he studied his digits in the dim light. He spread his fingers, and globs of shit cascaded down into the trash can. Maggots squirmed through his interdigital folds, and their warm, unctuous coating felt like noodles sliding between his fingers. "Oh shit oh shit oh shit!" Matt shook his hands. Feces and maggots flew everywhere.

"Well, why the hell did you close your eyes?" Jon slapped Matt in the back of the head. "Get the damn tapes!"

Matt gave a few spastic nods, then stared down into the trash can again. The tapes were just to the left. He reached in, grabbed the tapes, and hoisted them from the can. He shook off a few pieces of poop and maggots from them. "I got 'em, Jon!" Matt trembled with adrenaline and terror. "Now, let's get the hell out of here!"

Matt made a break for Bill's front lawn, and Jon grabbed him by the elbow. "Not so fast, Flash. You gotta go look in the window, remember? That was the

EZEKIEL KINCAID | 63

deal."

"Yeah, I don't wanna anymore." Matt's voice came out a little shaky. After being this close to the house, he was convinced Cory had been telling the truth.

"That wasn't the deal. You puss out now, and you see those guys across the street?" Jon swayed his head.

Matt wouldn't look. "I already got my hands covered in shit and maggots. Plus, I got the tapes," he said.

"That's cause you closed your eyes like a baby," Jon said. "Now, you see those guys over there? They are gonna keep pounding on you until you grow some balls. This is your chance to change things. Prove that you're not a pushover. We also need to know for sure if Cory was telling the truth." Jon placed both hands on Matt's shoulders and turned him toward Craddock's house. "Now go. I'll be right here hiding behind the trash can."

Matt didn't make a sound. He licked his lips, then took a deep breath. "Okay," he said as he exhaled. He handed Jon the tapes, rolled his neck, then took his first step towards the house. He found his legs were more cooperative and started into a fast walk. He journeyed across the yard to Craddock's window, keeping his sight fixated on the house.

Jon knelt behind the trash can and watched. He heard Matt's soft footsteps fade as he darted across the grass. Matt approached the rotting porch and stopped. He glanced over his shoulder at Jon, and Jon gave him a thumbs up. Feeling confident, Matt placed a foot on the first step.

The wood held steady and didn't make a squeak.

Matt paused and looked down at the wood, waiting for it to give way under him. He rocked back and forth, pushing with his toes. Solid. He stared at the window and stepped off the porch.

"Matt," Jon asked in a whisper yell. "What are you doing?"

Matt turned away from the house and faced Jon. "I can't," he whispered back to Jon.

"Dammit, Matt. Yes you can, now go."

"No." Matt took a step towards Jon.

"Yes, dammit. Go."

Matt took a centering breath. "Okay. Okay."

Matt did an about face and turned back to the house. He had a bad feeling about this—no, a terrible feeling. "God, help me. Jesus Christ, protect me," Matt prayed and proceeded up the steps. This time, the board gave a loud moan. Matt froze, baring his teeth in angst.

Jon flinched, ducking behind the trash can.

Matt's face fell long, and his eyes bulged behind his thick glasses. His blond hair waved as a howling gust of wind blew through the porch. Jon thought Matt would piss his pants, but he remained steadfast. The boys waited in the darkness of the night for Craddock to come out and catch them, putting an end to their lives and the entire adventure.

Nothing happened. All was clear.

Matt took slow, light steps over to the window and inspected it. Cracks meandered down the glass in several places, and the wood around it was chipped and rotting. Matt curled his lip. "Nasty," he whispered, then he pressed his face against the glass.

"What do you see?" Jon asked, standing tip-toed.

Matt waved for him to shush.

Matt's head moved back and forth, trying to get a better view. He then cupped his hands around the side of his face and peered through the glass. The humid summer air along with his heavy breathing fogged up his glasses and the window. Matt pulled back and took his glasses off. He wiped them with the bottom of his shirt, then placed them back on. Next, he used his forearm to wipe the fog off the window. He cupped his hands again, putting his face back to the glass. Matt stood there staring into the abyss.

A flash of light through the window.

A scream.

Loud popping noises.

Matt jerked back in horror, dread pulsating through all his limbs. His face contorted, and he clasped his jaw shut, trying to hold back a terrified yell. Matt dropped on his butt, rolled to all fours, and scurried like a rat off the porch.

"Oh shit, oh shit, oh shit." Matt said as he crawled onto the walkway. "He's gonna kill me!" He leaped to his feet and broke out in a full sprint.

Jon stepped out from behind the trash can and moved closer to get a better view of the window.

Craddock's face emerged from the dark, pressing onto the glass. His cheek mashed against it, making wrinkling lines across his profile. The whites of his eyes glowed a dingy yellow, like a smoker's teeth, and saliva dripped from his open mouth. Jon saw his mouth move, mumbling something. He didn't know what Craddock said, but he could tell he was madder than a nest of hornets.

Jon peered over his shoulder at Matt. He was already out of the driveway and turning onto the street. Jon's stomach turned in on itself and his entire body burned with the tingling sensation of fear.

Oh shit, oh shit, oh shit, Jon thought. He saw us! He fucking saw us! Jon looked back at the house. No one was in the window. Where the hell did Craddock go?

A door slammed.

Startled, he turned in the direction of the noise. Emerging from the shadows of the carport was a man in a red, hooded robe. His face stayed hidden in the darkness, and the size of his frame said he was well over six feet.

"Stop," he yelled at them.

The man's voice unnerved Jon. It tied his guts in knots, then untied them, again and again. He swore the goosebumps emerging from his flesh would burst through his skin like in the movie with the alien.

"Oh fuck," Jon said. He turned to run away, and Craddock slapped a hand against the window. Out of the corner of his eye, Jon thought he saw a bloody scalp with black hair snaking through Craddock's thin fingers.

"Bill, Terry, Dup! Run! Run, dammit," Jon screamed, running past the trash can. He caught a faint whiff of the old person and rotting potted meat smell. He sprinted through the grass, the rubbing sound of his sneakers amplified in his ears.

The man in the red robe was in a full pursuit of Jon and Matt.

"Come back here, you nosey little bastards," the man screamed.

"Matt," Jon yelled. "Let's meet at our spot!"

Matt gave a thumbs up. He dashed past Terry, Bill, and Chase. "He is after us! Go to our spot! Now!"

They turned their heads in a simultaneous motion and watched Matt fly by, then looked at Jon. The man in the red robe was closing the distance.

"Shit, dudes, run," Bill yelled at Chase and Terry.

They leaped off the porch and hauled ass to their secret hideout. All the boys ran in different directions, with Jon headed toward the main road.

Matt decided to take the long way and ran out the front of the neighborhood. He glanced over his shoulder. No one pursued him. "Dammit," he said. "That means he's after Jon." Feeling safer, Matt slowed his sprint to a jog. Don't stop, he told himself. Who knows if more of those red-robed fuckers are on their way.

The man in red gained on Jon. He had to think of

something fast. He was halfway to their spot, and he didn't want this asshole finding their hideout. They would kill him. Jon was certain of it. People like that didn't fuck around. His lungs burned, his legs ached, and his heart hammered against his breastbone. He had never run this fast or hard in his life.

Jon paused near the edge of Hooper Road. Cars zoomed past, their headlights blinding him. He squinted out into the road, listening as one vehicle after another rumbled by him. He did the only thing he could think of in that moment. Jon ran out into oncoming traffic.

The lady driving the blue truck saw Jon with not a second to spare. She slammed on her brakes. The tires screeched and left smears of black rubber as the truck tried to stop. The bright headlights disoriented Jon, but he didn't stop running. He heard the truck. He heard the squeal of the brakes. He heard the screaming tires … and mentally prepared himself for the impact.

The driver didn't have time to swerve. Jon was a fleeting shadow dancing across her windshield. The left tire grazed the back of Jon's heel as his foot was mid-air, just before the sole met the pavement. Jon leaped towards the grass line near the edge of the road and rolled into the ditch, holding the tapes close to his body. He was damn lucky, and he knew it. He scurried to his feet, back soaked in muddy water, and busted ass to the chain link fence separating the high school from the road. He had avoided becoming an asphalt pancake and he thanked God for it under his heaving breaths.

The guy in the green jeep wasn't as lucky. The man in the red robe seemed to magically appear out of nowhere in the middle of the road. The driver pressed his brakes, but the laws of physics were already in motion, not to be denied. The red figure smashed into the hood of the vehicle and rolled onto the windshield. He smacked against it with a godawful thud. The impact tossed the man in red's flailing body back down the hood and onto the street.

Jon heard the crunching sound as human bones collided with automobile steel. His stomach swirled inside his gut, and bile rose up the back of his throat. He didn't puke, and he didn't stop running either. He leaped over the fence to the high school, sprinted across the track, and ran under the bleachers of the football stadium. He placed his hand on his knees, sucking wind. Jon stayed in that position until his breathing slowed. "Jesus Christ," he said between gulps of air. "You're okay. You're okay."

Jon's stomach cramped, and the churning sensation returned. This time, there was no holding back. His body heaved and he opened his mouth, releasing a steady flow of yellowish-orange vomit all over the ground. "Gah! Shit!" Jon yelled. He spat a few times, then wiped his mouth with the back of his arm. The smell of the regurgitated pizza and Orange Crush ascended into his nostrils. Jon curled his lip and stood erect. The images flashed through his mind in rapid succession. The lights. The truck. The world in chaos as he leaped into the ditch. The sounds replayed next, as if they were on a continuous loop. Screeching tires. Shattering glass. A human body smashing into glass and metal.

"He's dead," Jon gasped. "The fucker's dead." He

rested a palm against a metal pole under the bleachers. It was cool to the touch in spite of the blistering heat earlier in the day. Jon removed his hand and pressed his cheek against it. The touch of the cool metal refreshed his flushed face. Jon closed his eyes, focusing on his breaths. In … out … in … out … He repeated the mantra until the shivers left his body and his heart rate slowed. A bit more relaxed, Jon opened his eyes and removed his face from the pole. He eased forward towards the opening underneath the bleachers, one foot in front of the other, then stood at the edge and peeked out.

Jon watched the pandemonium across the street. Cars were stopped in the middle of the road, and people gathered around the dead body. Panicked screams reverberated through the night air, someone yelling to find a phone and call 911. Jon eased out from underneath the safety of the bleachers. He made a slow turn, faced his back towards the road and his front towards the edge of the woods behind the stadium. He stared down at the tapes in his hand.

Just go, Jon thought. Just get the hell out of here and go to the spot. What started as a fast walk evolved into a jog, and within seconds, Jon was sprinting through the field. About a minute later, he took his first step through the foliage and into the woods. The sound of sirens echoed through the night, and for the first time since Craddock's house, he felt safe.

The boys' secret hideout rested about fifty yards deep into the woods. It wasn't fancy but still a good place to hang out and build fires in the winter. Their spot was nothing more than a clearing in the forest. The branches of the surrounding trees hung over it like a canopy, several of them snaking down and almost touching the ground. The boys always said it looked like a tree cave.

Bill, Terry, and Chase were already there, awaiting Jon's arrival.

"Jon, where is Matt?" Terry asked. He stood in the middle of the hideout, waiting for an answer.

Currents of happiness and relief flowed over Jon's body. His friends were safe. A surreal feeling washed over him, as if having some weird out of body experience. He wanted to talk, to smile. To say anything. But all he could do was stare at his friends with an empty expression.

"What the hell happened?" Bill asked. He stood a few feet to Terry's left, arm resting on a thick branch.

Jon shook his head. "Don't know." It was an effort to speak. His words sounded hollow in his ears, as if someone else spoke them.

Matt came barreling through the entrance. He stumbled towards Jon, eyes bulging and chest expanding with heavy breaths.

"You fucking asshole, Jon! I can't believe you talked me into this!" Matt screamed. He made a fist and pounded on Jon's arm.

Jon didn't say a word. He grabbed Matt by the throat, knocked his legs out from under him, and rolled him on his stomach, then sat down on his back.

"Get off me, asshole! We gotta go," Matt shouted. His glasses sat crooked on his face and snot dripped from his nose.

"Why did we have to run here? What happened?" Bill asked.

Matt tried to buck Jon off.

"Calm down," Jon yelled.

"No!" Matt bucked again.

Jon linked his hands together and placed his palms under Matt's chin. He yanked back, holding Matt in a partial Camel Clutch.

Matt winced in pain and spoke through gnashed teeth. "I'm going to the police." Spittle dribbled out the sides of his mouth. "Now let me go!"

"Matt, what's gotten into you? And why was that guy chasing us?" Terry asked. He stepped around and stood in front of his brother.

"Why you flippin' out on us, dude?" Chase bent over and looked Matt in the eyes.

Jon held on tight.

Matt spoke again through clenched teeth. "Get the hell off of me and I'll tell y'all."

"You're not gonna run on us or try to hit Jon?" Bill asked.

"No."

Jon relaxed his grip and lifted his butt off Matt's back.

Matt dropped his chin to the ground, laying with his face buried in the grass. Jon stepped off and Matt rose to all fours, then sat with his legs crossed.

"Jon, what happened to the dude that was chasing you?" Chase asked.

"You heard the sirens?" Jon asked.

Chase nodded.

"I ran out in the middle of Hooper Road and he followed. I almost got hit by a car, but him? He wasn't so lucky."

Terry's jaw dropped.

Bill's eyes widened.

Chase shook his head.

"What the hell, Jon," Bill said. "Is he dead?"

"I don't know. I had to do something or he would have followed us here."

"Great, someone is dead because of us." Terry slapped his hands on his thighs and turned away from the group.

"Save it, Terry," Jon said and sat on the ground by Matt. "Matt, what'd you see in there?"

The goosebumps on Matt's arms were visible, almost the size of ant bites. He glared straight ahead with a hollow expression on his face and adjusted his glasses. He lifted his legs up, wrapped his arms around his knees, and rocked. "Police. We gotta call ..." He trailed off.

Jon leaned over and grabbed Matt around the ears, jerking his head around. "Look at me, dammit, and talk. What did you see?"

Matt's hyoid bone rose and fell several times before he could utter an intelligible word. "A girl," he said, tears forming in the corner of his eyes.

"Was she hot?" Chase asked. Terry turned around and punched him in the arm, hard. "Ow. What?"

"What about the girl?" Bill asked.

Matt took a deep breath, exhaled, and relayed what he saw. "She was hanging from the ceiling. Her hands were in chains above her head … Her hair was gone …"

Jon thought about the scalp he saw in the window of Old Man Craddock's. Terror bubbled beneath his skin and poked it like a million little needles. His mouth went dry, and a cold shudder rippled through his body.

Cory had been telling the truth.

"Blood was all over her face. Mouth! Eyes! Everywhere! People in red, hooded robes were with her. And there was this other guy wearing a black goat skull and black robe. He pulled out this big goat horn and … and sliced it right across the girl's stomach and oh God!" Matt's voice escalated.

Jon massaged Matt's neck. "Shhhhh. Keep it down. What happened next?"

"He gutted her, man. But that ain't the worst of it, man. Not by far." Matt bobbed his head, and the tears flowed, fogging up his glasses. He removed them and placed them on the grass. "He gutted her, but guts didn't fall out. That ain't what came out, man."

"What, Matt? What came out?"

Matt paused, shifting his sight to Jon. "Snakes. Piles and piles of fucking snakes just poured out of her and all over the floor. They just kept coming out of her, nonstop. And her face! Her fucking face!"

"Hey, hey, hey, calm down. What? What about her face?" Jon asked.

"They were peeling pieces of it off and feeding it to her!"

Jon glanced up at his friends. They didn't move. They looked frozen in time, like statues with a freaked-the-fuck-out look stitched into their faces—eyes like shot glasses and mouths open so wide Jon could have shoved his fist inside them.

Jon turned his attention back to Matt. "The light and the popping noises, tell me about them."

"The light was a camera flash."

"Sick bastards," Jon whispered.

"The popping noises. Her bones. The girl started shaking and …"

"And what?" Jon asked.

Matt's head moved side to side in a slow motion. "I don't know. That's when Craddock appeared at the window."

Jon retrieved the tapes from the ground and inspected them. "We gotta see what's on these." He stood to his feet and brushed off his bottom.

"The hell we do," Bill disagreed. "We need to go to the cops. What Matt saw confirms what happened to my brother."

Jon rolled his eyes. "And what? Tell them we saw guys in robes gut a girl who bled snakes? Yeah, go ahead and see if they take you seriously. And your brother? Same thing! You think the police are gonna believe some woman melted all her skin off and turned into a monster? Wake the fuck up, Bill!"

"I don't know if I want to see what's on those tapes," Chase said.

"Me either." Terry put his hands in his pockets and stared at the ground.

Jon curled his lips and his eyebrows went to a point. "Are you shitting me? After what Matt just saw? How can you not want to see what's on the tapes? All of you are going soft. Besides, what if the evidence we need to prove that Mad Man Max is a murderer is on there? Then we'll have what we need. Then we can go to the cops."

"Why don't we just hand them the tapes?" Bill suggested.

"What if there's nothing on them but old television reruns? Then what?" Jon fired back. "No, I'm watching the tapes. If y'all are too chicken, that's fine."

"I wanna watch the tapes," Matt blurted.

The boys stopped arguing, and all eyes were now on Matt.

"What?" Terry asked. "You? After what you just saw? What the fuck is wrong with you?"

Matt stood up from the ground, wiped the grass off his clothes and face, then repeated what he said. "I wanna watch the tapes." He gave Jon a nod. "We need to see if there are any answers on them."

Jon smirked, then lit into Chase, Bill, and Terry. "Looks like little chicken shit over here has more balls than all three of you girls put together. Just wait till I tell everyone when we go back to school about how Matt here stepped up and the rest of you three ladies wimped out. My friends! Bill, Chase, and Terry. Step right up, folks, and see the ball-less wonders. The eunuchs of fear." Jon held his arms out and bowed.

"Shut up, Jon. Fine. We'll watch the stupid tapes." Bill placed his hands on his hips and spat.

"Terry? Chase?" Jon asked.

Neither said a word.

"I take that as a yes," Jon said.

"Where can we watch them? The only VCR we have is in the living room. My parents would be sure to walk in," Bill noted.

"Same here," Terry said.

"You idiots, stop beating around the bush. We all know I'm the only one who has a VCR in their room. We'll go back to my house and watch them," Jon said.

"How are we going to get to your house, Jon?" Chase asked.

"My dad would bring us," Bill said.

"Can we bring our bikes?" Terry asked.

The boys gave Terry a sideways glance.

"What? Why?" Chase asked.

"I love riding down Jon's long driveway and gravel road. Plus, it will give us something else to do," Terry said.

"How we gonna get them there?" Chase asked

"Yeah, that's fine, Terry," Bill said. "And we'll just strap them on top of my dad's Bronco."

Jon studied his friends with serious intent. "Guys," he said in a solemn tone. "Not a word to our parents about this."

They nodded in agreement.

"Good, now let's go back to Bill's," Jon said.

"We are gonna have to go to my house the back way so Craddock doesn't see us go in," Bill said. "Which means we are gonna have to cross the street where the dude was hit."

"Whatever," Chase said. "Let's just go."

The boys made their way out of the hideout. When they arrived at Hooper Road, the body was being loaded into an ambulance. The police were still questioning the drivers, and the boys heard the muffled conversations as they passed. Jon saw one of them raising his arms, then pointing across the street towards the school. The boys walked near the outside of the yellow tape, all of them trying not to stare at the pool of blood where the man was hit.

"I hope the asshole is dead," Jon muttered.

"Me too," Matt said.

"That's harsh, dude," Chase said.

"Yeah, well he wasn't chasing you trying to kill you," Jon said.

"And you didn't see what I saw," Matt said. "The bastard deserved it."

There was no more talk. They made the rest of their journey to Bill's house in silence. When they arrived, they talked to Bill's dad, loaded up the Bronco, and headed to Jon's house off Sullivan Road.

5

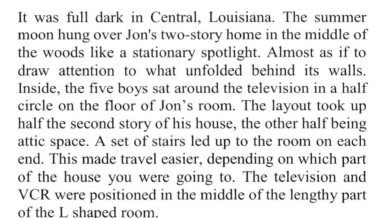

It was full dark in Central, Louisiana. The summer moon hung over Jon's two-story home in the middle of the woods like a stationary spotlight. Almost as if to draw attention to what unfolded behind its walls. Inside, the five boys sat around the television in a half circle on the floor of Jon's room. The layout took up half the second story of his house, the other half being attic space. A set of stairs led up to the room on each end. This made travel easier, depending on which part of the house you were going to. The television and VCR were positioned in the middle of the lengthy part of the L shaped room.

"I've got a foolproof plan in case my mom or dad comes in," Jon said.

"Same thing you did when we rented Faces of Death?" Bill asked.

"Yeah. We'll be able to hear them coming up the stairs or them opening the door. That will give me time to stop the tape and change the channel to TBS."

"And don't worry, fellas. Jon's parents won't find this the least bit suspicious since we watch TBS all the time when we're here." Bill assured Terry and Matt.

"Sounds good to me," Terry said.

"Good," Jon said. "Now where are the tapes?" He opened a Twinkie and devoured half of it in one bite.

"In my bag," Bill said through a mouthful of Moon Pie. He grabbed his electric blue Jansport and unzipped it. He reached in, grabbed the tapes, and tossed them on the green carpeted floor.

"What the hell is that?" Terry asked, eyes bugging behind his glasses.

Painted in the center of each tape with red paint was a symbol:

"I don't know. Didn't notice it before. With all the commotion and everything." Jon picked up one of the tapes and examined the symbol.

Chase grabbed another from the pile, flipping it over. "Looks like a Baphomet."

"It's not a Baphomet, Einstein. Baphomets are

upside down stars in a circle with a goat face in the star," Terry said, snatching the tape from Chase.

"Well, then what is it?" Chase swiped the tape back.

"Would you two idiots quit? If you wreck the tape, I'm gonna kick both your asses," Jon said, taking the tape from Chase. He studied the symbol one more time. "Holy shit! Guys!"

"What?" Bill asked. "What are you flipping out about now?"

"What did Cory say the symbol he saw on the wall looked like?" Jon asked.

Chase's eyes shot to the upper corner of his sockets, thinking. "Ummmm … he said it was a circle with some sort of triangle or star things in it, pushing outside the circle with some other lines through it."

Jon held up the tape, symbol facing his friends. "Kind of like this, maybe?"

Chase's eyes widened like someone stuck a finger up his ass. "Oh shit! Jon's right!"

"Holy hellballs," Bill said, wiping Moon Pie crumbs from his mouth. He swallowed and said, "That's gotta be the same symbol. I mean, it fits, right?"

"It sure does," Jon said. Jon's spirit soared on an adrenaline high. This was all too good. Cory's story. Craddock. The tapes. It was all coming together. They were on the verge of cracking this mystery wide open.

"Which one should we watch first?" Matt asked

and chugged his root beer.

"I don't think it matters," Bill said.

"Yeah, just put one in." Chase shoved a handful of chips in his mouth, making the last part of the sentence unintelligible.

Jon checked the reel. The tape had been rewound. He lifted the flap and blew a few times, making sure all the dust was removed. He looked around the room, spotting the towel he'd used that morning when he showered wadded up on the floor next to his bookshelf. He got to his feet, grabbed the towel, and wiped down the tape. He walked over to the VCR and popped it in. The VCR hummed, then made a clicking sound as it set the tape. Jon pushed the power button on the television and mashed PLAY on the VCR. He resumed his place on the floor.

Jon's pulse thumped so hard he heard it in his ears. His palms turned sweaty, and the back of his throat tickled. He knocked back another few sips of Coke, attempting to remedy the sensation. The intricate mix of dread and anticipation surged through his veins, making all his extremities feel coated in cement. He glanced around at his friends. They stared at the screen, immobilized. Chase's bag of chips trembled in his hand, and Terry's cheeks were flushed. Bill sat stoic, stiff and unbending. They were all either scared shitless or enthralled, Jon didn't know which.

The boys gazed at the screen, then at each other, sharing anxious looks.

Yeah, scared shitless, Jon thought. Just like me.

There was nothing but static and white noise for the first few seconds. The picture danced, and the scenery came into focus in waves.

It was nighttime, and the light on the camera revealed a railroad trestle—old, rusted, ominous. Underneath the trestle was a road. There were a few more seconds of the bridge, then more static and white noise. The film came back into focus. A close-up of the side of the trestle. There were words spray painted across the front of the wood running underneath the railroad tracks.

The boys angled closer to the television.

The words read "Welcome To The Gates Of Hell." The camera shook; the only noise was the lens cap slapping against the mic. Then there was heavy breathing. The camera zoomed back, then focused in on the pillars underneath the track. Symbols were painted on them, symbols like the ones on the tapes. The camera panned to the left, then pointed down. Spray painted on the road before the trestle was the phrase "Go back now" along with more satanic graffiti on the asphalt.

Then nothing but more static and white noise.

The picture came into focus. The view was from below the trestle. Rays of sunlight illuminated what was under the bridge. It looked to be either early in the morning or late in the evening. Countless cats hung by ropes underneath the trestle. Some were dead; some were alive. A hand holding a revolver appeared on the screen, pointing towards the cats.

Bam! Bam! Bam!

Three successive shots rang out.

The boys jumped. Chase's chips flew out of his bag, and Jon's Coke sloshed into his lap. The head of the cat closest in view of the camera burst open as if it were a furry melon. A laugh bellowed from the television, sending waves of cold shivers through the boys' souls.

Then, more static as the screen jumped.

The next scene was from atop of the trestle on the tracks. It was nighttime again, and the camera faced one end of the railroad. The dim light revealed tracks seeming to lead into a deep abyss of woods. The camera panned down. Tied to the tracks in chains was a man. His mouth was taped shut, and blood flowed from his nose, coating the gray tape. His eyes bulged and he let out muffled screams.

A deafening whistle blew.

The camera panned to the other end of the tracks.

A bright light appeared, racing through the dark. The camera went back to the man. He convulsed and screamed. The camera shook as whoever held it walked past the man and down one side of the embankment. The next scene was filmed from there.

The camera angle showed the screaming man in the bottom of the screen with the thundering train at the top. It sped through the night air, blaring its whistle. As the train approached, the sound of shaking tracks and spinning driving wheels drowned out the man's pleas.

The train was a roaring lion, and the man was its

prey. Steel met flesh, and physics took over. The man exploded into a cloud of red. The locomotive rumbled past the camera, and a lunatic's laugh resounded from the television.

The tape glitched and jumped as a distorted image appeared on screen. The VCR buzzed and hummed as the automatic tracking set in. A close-up of a black goat skull appeared on the screen for about ten seconds, followed by more white static.

The boys didn't move. They didn't speak. They just gazed at the white lines scampering across the television. The same expression was on each face: eyes like silver dollars, eyebrows raised to full attention, and mouths so wide you could pop a baseball in there.

"What the fuck did we just watch?" Chase asked. His chip bag crinkled as he removed a chip. He put it in his mouth and crunched away.

All the boys turned their heads towards Chase in a slothful, fluid motion. Their faces all said the same thing. It was a "how the hell can you be eating after what we just saw" look. Chase didn't notice. He kept munching on his chips.

"Do you think it was fake?" Matt asked. He stared down at his root beer, playing with the tab.

"No way," Bill said. "You can't fake that."

Matt popped the tab of his can.

"Where was that? You think it's around here? That bridge?" Terry asked

"Yes," Jon said. He was anxious, so he grabbed a packet of Zebra Cakes from the pile of goods lying in

EZEKIEL KINCAID | 87

the middle of their circle. He bit it open, spit out the piece of wrapper, and dumped one out in his hand. He now understood why Chase could eat during all this. His nerves were on end, and he didn't know what else to do.

The crinkling wrapper snapped Chase out of his daze. "Oh, bullshit, Jon. You're just trying to scare us."

Jon devoured his Zebra Cake in one bite. He gulped the rest of his Coke, wiped his lips with the back of his arm, and belched.

"You mean y'all don't recognize it?" Jon asked, crushing his Coke can. He looked at them, expecting recollection. "That's the trestle at the end of Frenchtown Road. The one where all those high school kids got murdered three years ago."

"No it's not," Terry said, waving his hand at Jon.

"Yes it is," Jon said and threw his crushed can at Terry.

Terry swatted it away right before it smacked his face. "The fuck it is; you are trying to be an ass."

"I am not," Jon said, jumping to his feet. "How could you say that, you Sega Genesis sellout?'

"Bullshit, Jon," Terry said. "You know I still prefer Nintendo."

"Ha ha," Chase laughed and pointed at Terry. "Sega sellout."

"Would y'all stop," Bill said. "I remember hearing my parents talking about something like this."

"Yeah, I do too," Jon said. "I overheard my parents

talking about it and the murders. It was all the urban legend stuff about Frenchtown Road. My mom said those stories have been around since the early nineteen eighties."

"Yeah, I remember some of them," Chase said. "There was the one about parking your car under the bridge and turning it off. Then it won't start."

"Yeah, and there is another one about a guy who hung himself out there. People still report seeing his ghost," Jon said.

Chase looked at Jon, snapping his fingers. "Yeah, yeah. Wasn't there also one about a little girl who got run over by a train on the trestle?"

"Yep." Jon nodded. "And when a train comes, you can still hear her scream." Jon paused, thinking, then said, "But the most famous one is about the cult. And this is where the murders started. This urban legend popped up in nineteen eighty-two. Two high school kids went out to the bridge to test the legend about the car. No one ever saw them or heard from them again. Rumors about them being murdered by a cult started right after."

"What does that have to do with the murders that happened three years ago?" Terry asked.

"Well," Jon said, "back in nineteen eighty-seven, a group of high school friends went out to visit the trestle and camp out in the woods. They wanted to see if the urban legend about the cult was fact or fiction. They were picked off one by one. The police found a few of the bodies, but not all of them. They questioned everyone on the road, even Theodosia. They found no evidence of the body and no signs of occult activity whatsoever."

Jon grabbed another Coke from the pile, then sat back down. "And one more thing. You know how I know it is the bridge?"

Matt traced his lips with his finger. "How?"

"I've been out there," Jon said.

"What the …" Chase's voice faded.

"You're full of it," Bill said, throwing his Moon Pie wrapper at Jon. It went about two feet, then boomeranged back to Bill.

"Nah-ah." Terry waved his hand. "No way."

"I believe you, Jon," Matt said. "When?"

"It was about two and a half years ago, not too long after the murders happened. Y'all remember my older cousin, Emily?"

Chase snickered. "You bet we do," he said. "She's hot! Nice tits."

The rest of the boys smiled in agreement.

Jon rolled his eyes and continued. "Yes, we are all aware everyone wants to bone my cousin. Anyway, she was babysitting me one day after school. I don't remember why. She wanted to run to Video Co-op off Greenwell Springs. Said they had the only copy in town of some B movie horror flick she wanted to see."

"Oh, which one?" Chase asked

Bill punched him in the arm, and the others shushed him.

"I don't know, moron, that's not the point," Jon said. "The point is, after we went to the video store, on the way home, she asked me if I wanted to take a ride down Frenchtown Road and see where those murders took place."

"What'd you say?" Chase crisscrossed his legs.

The boys groaned with frustration, and Bill punched Chase in the arm again, harder.

"Ow-a," Chase said, rubbing the spot where Bill belted him.

"I said yes, dumbass," Jon said. "We drove to the end of the road and got out to see it. It looked just like it does in those videos. The markings. The symbols. All of it. I'll never forget. Eerie as hell. Most scared I've ever been in my life. You can feel the evil there, just resting over the place."

"Did they ever catch the people who murdered those kids?" Bill asked.

"No," Jon said.

Bill's face lit up. "Oh shit. Do y'all realize what this means?" he said. "We have to finish those tapes! What if there are clues on them? Clues that will lead to the killers?"

Jon snapped his fingers. "Bill's right," he said. "We gotta watch the others and see if there are clues. And I guarantee what Cory saw is connected to all this in some way."

Terry grew uneasy at the direction the conversation headed. "I don't know, fellas," he said. "I think we should just hand the tapes over to the police and be done with it."

"You pussy," Matt huffed.

Ohs and damns rang forth from the boys.

Chase laughed the hardest. "You know you're a puss when Matt calls you out!"

Terry flipped Chase off. "Shut up, Dup."

"I don't know, Dup," Bill said. "Matt did go get the tapes."

"Meh," Chase waved his hand. "Matt's just a one hit wonder. He will always be a puss."

"Kiss my ass, Dup. I didn't see you volunteer," Matt said.

"Stop." Jon emptied the other Zebra Cake into his hand. "All in favor of watching the other tapes and looking for clues, raise your hand." Jon lifted his hand gripping the cake.

Chase, Bill, and Matt shot their hands up. Terry rolled his eyes and scowled, then eased his in the air.

"Good. Now that that's settled, let's play the other tape." Jon shoved the Zebra Cake in his mouth and picked up the second tape. He flipped it open and blew crumbs out his mouth all into the inside. "Ah, dammit," Jon screamed, specks of yellow cake dribbling from his lip.

"Dude, what the hell? You're gonna fuck up the tape," Bill said, holding open his hands.

Jon swallowed and wiped his face with the back of his arm. "Sorry. A little on edge." He inspected the inside of the tape, gently blowing the remaining remnants of Zebra Cake from the tape, then ejected the previous tape, put the new one in, and pushed PLAY.

The picture on the screen came into focus. It was a large white farmhouse with faded green shutters and a wrap-around porch. The camera panned to the right, turning a full 180 degrees. Stone ruins lay in the middle of the hilly landscape. Thunder rumbled and rain poured, then, white static.

The next image came into focus, a felt painting with a dark green background filling much of the canvas. The portrait of a woman with auburn hair wearing a black dress contrasted with the green backdrop. But she had no face. The camera stayed focused on the picture. Fifteen seconds passed. Thirty. One minute.

"This one's retarded," Chase said.

"Shut up," Jon said. "Clues. We're looking for clues. Stay focused."

Two minutes passed, and the camera still remained focused on the painting. Jon squinted, leaning in toward the television.

"What?" Bill asked.

"I think something's appearing in the painting." Jon pointed.

All the boys moved closer.

"Yeah, two little red circles where the eyes should be," Bill said.

The two red dots increased in circumference. They

grew abnormally large for her face, then stopped. Another red dot formed in place of the mouth. It expanded, covering the space where her mouth and jaw should be, and ceased.

"That's messed up," Chase said.

A loud popping noise crackled from the television, followed by the three dots spewing red liquid. It dripped out the holes and down the face of the painting.

"No, Dup. That's messed up," Terry said.

The familiar white static paraded across the screen again. Coming into view next was a crypt. When the picture settled, the boys saw it with more clarity. The camera light revealed a brown and rusty crypt. Grass grew halfway up the stone columns, with vines encasing the backside. The camera zoomed to the top of the entryway. Etched in the stone was a name.

"Theodosia Whitfield? Who's that?" Chase asked.

No one answered.

White static.

"This is some weird shit," Terry said. He grabbed the box of Twinkies from the pile and fetched one, eyes still locked on the television.

"Holy shit, what is that! What the fuck is that?" Bill pointed at the screen.

The camera had panned back, capturing an entire room in its frame. On the left was a glass-encased shelf filled with dolls. In the back of the room was a large crimson wardrobe. In the middle of the room was a bed. A few feet from the bed sat a brown rocking chair.

In the rocking chair sat … a thing. A thing so gross and terrifying, the boys couldn't look away.

The creature's body was a charcoal color. Its skin flowed thick and leathery like rustling sails, and it had no eyes. Instead, protruding out of its eye sockets were horns. They curved around the creature's head and sat above its bat-like ears. Rows of jagged teeth, like glass, lined its mouth, looking as if someone crammed them in there. The creature rocked back and forth in the chair, humming. Its voice grated, sounding like rocks being thrown around in a blender. The tune it hummed reminded the boys of a lullaby. The creature raised one bony hand off the armrest and waved at the camera. It's emaciated finger sliced through the air, exposing bulging knuckles and long, black fingernails.

The second tape ended.

The boys sat in silence, terror settling over them like a heavy fog. The only noise in the room was the rewinding of the tape. The tape clicked, and the VCR ejected it.

The sound of Bill swallowing his spit came next, followed by his shaking voice. "Was that … y'all think it was real? … 'cause it sure looked real."

Jon mumbled something.

"Huh?" Terry said, cocking his head to the side. He stared at Jon for clarification. "What did you say?"

"Theodosia Whitfield," Jon said with a whisper.

"Yeah," Bill said. "The name on the crypt. You also mentioned it earlier. You know what it means?"

Jon gave a slow nod as if his head was being pulled

up and down by a string. "Yeah, I do." Jon's eyes glazed over, and he ran his tongue over his dry lips. He'd made the connection. How could he have not seen it until now? "Theodosia Whitfield," he whispered. "The witch who won't die."

"Dude, what are you talking about?" Bill's expression was one of sheer terror. His skin was as white as a bedsheet, and he picked at his fingernails.

Jon's vision never left the screen. "Theodosia Whitfield. She revived the Tetromet cult."

"The what?" Chase asked.

"The Tetromet cult," Jon said.

"What's a Tetromet?"

Jon didn't answer. He stayed fixated on the television.

Terry waved at him. "Hello?"

Terry's voice sounded distant in Jon's ears. "He's more evil and powerful than Satan himself," Jon said. "He used to be the cherub that guarded the tree of life."

"You mean, like, the tree in the Garden of Eden?" Matt said, his nose wrinkling under the weight of his glasses.

Jon's head movement gave affirmation. "The cherub got pissed when he found out plans had been made to open the tree back up to humanity. To give them access to it and redemption. But these plans didn't include Lilith. He was in love with her, but God said she was an abomination because of her mating with Satan—"

"Now wait just a damn minute," Chase said and crossed his arms. "A human having sex with the devil? What is this, angel porn? And who is Lilith?"

"Angel porn," Matt said and chuckled. "Good one, Dup."

"Shut up, Matt. We already determined earlier today you don't know what that is," Terry said.

"Hey," Jon yelled. "Cut the shit and listen. It isn't angel porn, got it?" He scowled at Chase. "Lilith was made before Eve. She was Adam's first wife. She was too domineering and violent. She left Adam and had sex with Samael—"

"Who is Samael? And come on, how is this not angel porn?" Chase asked.

"Samael was supposedly Satan in Jewish legend," Jon said. "Anyway, because of Lilith's actions, God kicked her out and she was an abomination. God then made Eve for Adam. And the cherub and Lilith ended up falling in love."

"Then what happened?" Terry asked.

"Well, since the cherub loved Lilith and was pissed God wasn't going to give her redemption, he let out his anger on God, saying it wasn't fair that the rest of humanity could be redeemed but not Lilith." Jon paused to see if any of the other four dipshits were going to interrupt again. They didn't. "God disagreed. So then, the cherub became everything he stood against—rebellious and hateful. He used his flaming sword to cut the tree of life down and chop it to pieces. He smashed all the fruit as well."

Jon paused and took a sip of his drink. He swallowed, then said, "God judged him and took away his angel form. He lost his position as guardian cherub and was transformed into this terrible thing. It's head, man. It's supposed to be like this big freaking black goat skull. Its body is furry like a cat, complete with claws. But the part that really makes me wanna crap my pants? His tail. It's this big-ass snake with this huge head." Jon held his hands up and spread them apart, emphasizing the size of the head. "He was turned into the Tetromet … and he was pissed. Michael and some of the other angels went and killed Lilith. So then the Tetromet took her body and planted a seed from one of the fruits from the tree of life inside it."

"What happened next?" Terry asked.

"A new tree grew. His tree," Jon said.

"Why did he plant another tree? For what?" Chase asked

Jon's gaze left the television, shifting onto his friends. "The tree became his physical connection to our world. The tree … it's like his life source. The more branches that grow on his tree, the more powerful he becomes. When he gets enough branches, he'll have the strength to manifest in physical form. When he does …" Jon glared hard at them, narrowing his eyes.

"What, man? Come on, spit it out," Bill said.

"Game over," Jon said.

"What do you mean, game over?" Matt asked.

"Armageddon. End of the world. The death of the human race," Jon said.

"So just how does he get these branches?" Bill asked, a smirk draped across his face. He was skeptical as hell. Jon's story sounded like nothing more than a horror twist on a Sunday School lesson.

"That's where the cult comes in," Jon said. "Anyone who is either sacrificed to the Tetromet or killed in his name by one of the cult members? Their soul descends to the Tetromet, and he devours them. When he does, a branch forms on his tree, and he is one step closer to physical manifestation."

"Okay, let's say your story is true," Bill said. "Where does Theodosia Whitfield fit into all this?"

"Theodosia," Jon said. "She revived the Tetromet cult in the early 1800s. Her father was a professor at UNC in North Carolina. He taught and wrote on ancient people and religions. When she was young, Theodosia became fascinated with her dad's work. While looking through her father's stuff, she came across two ancient documents that he translated." Jon held up his hand, extending his pointer and middle finger. "The Book of Saul and The Gospel of Thaddaeus. Both these books tell stories about the Tetromet."

"The former cherub?" Matt asked.

"Yeah," Jon said. "The Tetromet supposedly appeared to Theodosia and told her to start killing in his name. He also gave her immortality. She can't be killed, or if she is, she comes back to life. It was something like that. I can't remember all the details."

"How did he get the name Tetromet, and what does it mean?" Matt asked.

"His name," Jon said. "It's some combination of Latin and Hebrew. It means 'the dreadful death.' From the stories I've heard, the name fits."

"Wow," Matt gasped. "Fucking unbelievable."

"Where'd you hear all this crap?" Chase asked.

"It's not crap, idiot. Have you not been watching?" Jon asked. He grabbed the last tape. "Emily. She told me some about it. But most of it I heard from Pastor Moore."

"What, you just showed up to his office one day and said, hey, Pastor, tell me about all those kids that were murdered?" Chase asked.

"No," Jon said. "It was one Sunday night after church. We had the Moores over to eat dessert with us. Pastor Moore and my dad went off to the living room to talk. I was in the kitchen halfway listening. Until I heard them mention Frenchtown Road. Then I really started to listen. It was something about how kids were going out there again. Pastor Moore said it was dangerous, then went into everything I told y'all."

The boys studied Jon, taking in everything he said and weighing it. He was a lot of things, but a liar wasn't one of them.

"Anything else?" Bill asked.

"Theodosia is the leader of the cult," Jon said. "She's still alive. And I bet that she's the witch who lives in the last house on the left at the end of Frenchtown Road."

"Nice story, Jon, but honestly, I think you're full of shit." Bill raised his Dr. Pepper to Jon and took a sip.

A liar, Jon was not. But a bullshitter? He had pulled stunts like this before.

"This reminds me of the time you tried to convince us that you had a Critter as a pet," Bill said.

"Yeah," Chase agreed. "I believed you for, like, a week. Until Bill told me it was just a racoon you had trapped in a box."

"Well I believe you, Jon," Matt said.

"You still believe in Santa Claus," Terry said.

Chase and Bill chuckled.

Jon flared his nostrils. "I'm not full of shit," he said. "The symbols, the cult, and the tapes. Cory's story. They're all connected. And Mad Man Max is neck deep in it all."

Chase's mind processed everything Jon had said. He finally connected the dots and stopped denying the obvious—what they saw on the tapes, what Matt saw at Mad Man Max's house. "I believe you, Jon." Chase said, then looked at Bill.

"You flip-flopping already, Dup?" Bill asked.

"Come on, man, use your head and stop being a chicken shit," Chase said. "The tapes? What Matt saw? The murders and what Jon told us? Your fucking brother?"

"I'm not a chicken shit, you chicken shit," Bill said and flipped him off. "I just want proof."

"Proof? Proof?" Matt's voice cracked. "What the

hell have we been watching?"

"Matt's right, Bill," Chase said. He looked at Jon. "Again, I believe you."

"Me too," Terry said.

"So do I," Matt said.

"Fine. Why don't we just go ahead and play the last tape," Bill said. His demeanor softened under the disapproving scowls of his friends. This was the typical MO for Bill. He'd bitch and complain for a while, then throw his hat in the ring later.

"Good," Jon said. Before he put in the next tape, he craned his neck and said, "One more thing. That creature we saw on the last tape? Looks a hell of a lot like the one Cory described." He popped the last tape into the VCR and played it, then sat down, waiting for the tape to reveal its new scenes of horror.

The boys processed Jon's last statement while waiting for what the tape would reveal. Bill's skin crawled, cold and frosty, as if his clothes were made of ice. The connection Jon made about the creature was downright bone chilling. It was as if Jon's voicing of the revelation sucked all the light and hope out of the room.

All the boys sensed it. It was like a canopy of darkness spread out over the room, shielding them from God and everything good in the universe. It was just them, the tapes, and their fear, cuddled up together and submerging into the horror.

Matt adjusted his butt on the floor and pushed his glasses up.

Terry gnawed on his fingernails.

"Don't spit those on my floor," Jon said.

"I'm not," Terry said.

Chase opened another bag of chips.

Jon crisscrossed his legs and gazed at the screen.

The tape glitched, then the film came into focus. It was nighttime, and the picture bobbed up and down. Whoever held the camera was running. The only thing the boys could see on the screen was flashes of black and yellow. They heard harrowing laughter followed by screams. The person filming stopped running and settled the camera. A field came into view, with grass about waist high. The camera panned to the right and focused on a blue metal warehouse with white rolling doors. Then there was a scraping sound as someone raised one of the doors.

The picture shook as the cameraman ran inside. He steadied the camera and spoke. "Stupid sons a bitches. They think it's all a fucking game. They'll see." The side of a whiskey bottle appeared on screen as the cameraman knocked some back. The label read "Evan Williams."

Jon leaped to his feet. His chest expanded as he took heavy breaths, and his hands hung by his side. He struggled to get his words out, but when he did, they came so fast not even he understood what he said at first. "Shit oh shit oh shit. Fucking shit fucking fuck me shit. Fucking look!" Jon pointed at the screen. "Craddock! The camera. Him. Fucking Mad Man fucking Max! He's the one with the camera. The one who's been filming!"

The rest of the boys looked up at Jon. The color left their faces, and their eyes bulged. The tingle of fear snaked its way up into the backs of their throats. They didn't want to believe Jon. They didn't want to believe what they saw on the tape. Their twelve-year-old minds wanted to go back to Nintendo games and wrestling. But they couldn't. Mad Man Max came through loud and in living color.

"How? How do you know?" Bill asked as his eyes darted back and forth from Jon to the television. It was a dumb question. He knew; he just wanted someone to make the nightmare end, to slap him in the face or tell him it was all a joke.

Jon's breathing was still heavy, and his hand stayed pointed at the television. "The voice," he said. "That phrase 'sons a bitches.' He says it all the time. And the whisky bottle. Evan Williams. That's what he was drinking when he came out to the trashcan earlier."

"Oh, come on, Jon," Bill said. He gave rapid blinks, wrestling off the fear squeezing his heart. "You don't know a damn thing about whiskey and whiskey bottles."

"I do too," Jon said. "My dad drinks Evan Williams sometimes. I recognize the bottle. That's Craddock, Bill, and stop trying to fucking deny it!" Jon lowered his arm, then bowed up to Bill.

"Okay, okay," Bill said and eased off. He remembered the bottle of Evan Williams in the Benson's kitchen pantry. He had snuck a drink out of it last weekend.

"Shut up, you two pussies, and look," Chase said, motioning with his head at the screen.

Jon relaxed his body at the sound of Chase's voice, but his insides flexed hard. He didn't want to see any more of the tape.

Jon's gaze left Bill and returned to the screen. Bill's argumentative spirit subsided, and he closed his eyes. He heard rustling noises from the television, and it took everything in him not to turn around and shut it off.

Terry caught a glimpse of Bill out of the corner of his eye. "Don't puss out now," he said. "This is the last tape."

Bill jumped at Terry's voice, popping his eyes open. "I'm not, asshole," Bill said and rolled his shoulders. "Fuck you."

A naked woman lay on a stone slab, tied down with rope. An old lady sat on her, straddling her midsection. The old lady's white, wiry hair was pulled up in a ponytail and rested on the top of her head. Animal skins covered her chest, midsection, and hips. People dressed in red, hooded robes surrounded the stone slab. The old lady whipped her head back and started to chant.

The boys heard each utterance with clarity. The words made Jon's stomach turn like he'd swallowed a miniature tilt-a-whirl. The chant came through the speaker, and every follicle of Jon's hair felt as if it had been submerged in ice water.

"All ye who breathe,

Who walk in the night.
Away from the sun,
And beyond the light.

In the realm of darkness you go,
Descending into the pain below.

In here, you'll find suffering and fear,
As your life is taken and your blood is smeared.

Down here, you'll face the Tetromet,
Who will draw from you, your dying breath.
Goat, feline, and serpent, all three.
He is our god, our trinity.

So close your eyes,
And hear our epithet.
As you prepare to meet,
The entity called Tetromet."

The old lady raised her arms above her head. In her hands, she held a large goat horn. She snarled, bringing it down into the naked woman's chest. The camera picked up the crunching sounds, and they bellowed forth from the television. Blood spurted from the wound, all over the woman and the old lady. The young woman gasped as if she was trying to suck all the air out of the room. The old lady howled in laughter, opening her mouth to reveal yellow, infected teeth. Then the picture faded to white.

Chase's hand was paused mid motion. He was putting a chip to his mouth before the scene started. The chip never made it to its destination.

Bill closed his eyes. He didn't want to watch any more. He couldn't get the scene nor the sounds out of his head. And for some reason, he still thought about the whiskey bottle.

Terry sat shaking his head. He tried to tell himself it wasn't real and the tapes were fake. His mind didn't know what to make of the last scene. It seemed to hang in limbo, the in-between state of the mind that is like a mental glitch, where what was witnessed resides in the forefront like a paused movie screen.

Matt took off his glasses and ran his hands down his face, the sweat accumulating in his fingers and palms. He gazed down into his hands and wiped the perspiration onto his legs.

Jon was fascinated. His lips were locked in a half smile. He knew they didn't have enough evidence to put Craddock away, but his mind churned with a plan.

"Guys, I don't think we should—" Bill's voice was interrupted by the television.

In the next segment, there was nothing but darkness. Then the clatter of someone messing with the camera. The light on the camcorder turned on, and trees filled the screen. Whoever filmed stood deep in a forest, probably the one down Frenchtown Road. The camera pointed down. A pile of bloody body parts, stacked about three feet high and six feet in diameter, appeared on screen. The person holding the camera rotated it so they could film their face. Only, it wasn't the face of a person. Staring at the boys through the screen was a large, black goat skull. Whoever operated the camera wore one as a mask. The person moved to remove the skull, and as the skull lifted just above their chin, the camera stopped recording.

"Ah shit! Come on," Chase yelled at the television.

"Doesn't matter," Jon said. "We all know it's Craddock."

"So, let's go to the cops," Bill said.

"No." Jon stood up. "We don't have hard evidence. All we have is a whiskey bottle and a curse word."

"So, we know it's him," Terry said.

"Yeah, we know. But this isn't enough to convince the cops," Jon said.

"So, what do we do?" Bill stood to his feet, facing Jon.

Jon stared at the floor, shaking his head. He knew his friends would balk at what needed to be done. He said it anyway. "We need to go out there."

Before the boys could respond, they heard the thudding of footsteps coming up the stairs.

"Shit, the remote," Jon said. "Where is it?" He had forgotten where he had placed it.

"Behind you," Bill said.

Jon looked behind him and grabbed the remote. He pointed it at the television, stopped the tape, and turned on TBS.

"Tonight, on TBS," the narrator's voice echoed through the room.

"The tapes! Give me the other two tapes," Jon said, snatching the backpack off the floor.

Terry and Bill tossed the tapes to Jon. He slipped them into the backpack and zipped it, then tossed the backpack to the other side of the room and sat back down on the floor.

The door opened, and Jon's mom came in. "What's all the racket?" she asked. She was wearing a pink and white nightgown, and her blonde hair was still wet from the shower.

"Oh," Jon said, trying to act like they didn't have a plan to investigate a murder. "We're just excited about tonight's movies."

"Yeah," Bill said. "We've been waiting all week for this."

"What's on?" Mrs. Benson asked.

"Uhhhhh …" Jon said, staring at the screen. The commercials playing were for Motel Hell and Poltergeist. "Just some cheesy horror movies."

Jon's mom examined the boys with a keen eye. "Why do y'all look so nervous?"

"Well," Chase said, "we've never seen either of these movies, so we are wondering how scary they're going to be."

That was a lie. Chase, Bill, and Jon had seen each movie at least three times.

"You boys are gonna have nightmares. I don't want to hear about how y'all couldn't sleep tonight," Mrs. Benson said, laughing. She looked at Terry and Matt. "Is your mom okay with y'all watching stuff like this?"

"Oh sure," Terry lied. Their mom never let them watch scary movies. "We watch horror movies all the time."

Terry and Matt exchanged uncertain glances.

"Okay," Mrs. Benson said. She turned to walk out of the room, then paused. "Do y'all want me to make some popcorn?"

"No thanks, Momma," Jon said. "We have plenty to eat." He motioned with his head towards their pile of goods.

"I guess you do," Mrs. Benson said. "Let me know if y'all need anything."

"We will," Jon said.

Mrs. Benson left the room and headed down the stairs.

The boys sighed in relief.

"Up next …" The narrator's voice hung in the air. "Motel Hell."

Jon gazed at the television, giving mindless blinks while the clip of Rory Calhoon with the pig head and chainsaw played across the screen.

The rest of the boys joined him. No one wanted to think about what they saw on the tapes—no one but Jon.

Jon's eyes fluttered, and he shook his head. He snapped back into reality, remembering his plan. "We are gonna go out there to the end of Frenchtown Road," he said.

Jon's words drowned out the television, and Chase was the first to respond.

"Nope." Chase looked over at Jon and waved his hands. "Hell no. I'm out. What is wrong with you, Jon? You want us to go out there where some teenagers were murdered three years ago? And at night?" Chase leaped to his feet and tried to leave the room.

The other boys turned from the television and watched to see what Jon would do.

Was he going to lay Chase out? Like the one time Bill challenged Jon, and Jon picked him up like a rag doll and threw him across the room?

Jon stepped in front of Chase, blocking him from exiting the room. "Listen, Dup." He placed his hands on Chase's chest. "We gotta get more evidence. There's some out there. I know it. And those murders were three years ago. Nothing has happened since."

"Yeah," Chase said. "Because no one is fucking stupid enough to go out there at night."

Jon dropped his hands. The two boys stood inches apart, staring one another down. Chase's warm air settled on Jon's neck. He could smell the faint scent of

Doritos still lingering on Chase's breath.

Jon wanted to punch Chase across the jaw as his mind reminisced to last year when Chase felt brave, or stupid, enough to test him.

They were playing baseball during PE. Jon and Chase had been at each other for days. Chase was pitching, and Jon was at bat. Jimmy Campbell had told Chase not to fuck with Jon, but Chase didn't listen. His first pitch went right at Jon's midsection. Jon turned, and the ball collided with a hollow thud against his back.

"Oops," Chase had said. He shrugged his shoulders and punched his fist in his glove, then walked back to the mound. "Guess that one got away from me." He glanced over at Bill, who played shortstop.

"You're a damn dead man, Dup," Bill said.

Jon had taken the hit, then spun around, throwing his bat at the fence.

Jimmy Campbell was playing catcher, and he jumped to his feet. "Jon, be cool." He lifted his mask and tried to talk to Jon.

Jon flung off his batting helmet and got in Jimmy's face. "I'm good," Jon had said.

Coach Rodney jogged over to home plate with Jon and Jimmy.

"You okay, Jon?" he had asked.

Jon clenched his fist, then released. He looked at coach, then Jimmy. "Yeah," he said. "I'm good."

Coach Rodney walked away, and Jimmy pulled down his mask. Coach didn't see it, but Jimmy did. Jon walked to the fence to get his bat and eyed Chase. Chase had grabbed his crotch and mouthed "Suck it, faggot."

Jon was off like a track star. He tackled Chase at the mound and before anyone could break it up, Chase was bleeding from his nose and mouth.

Jon saw the same fear churning in Chase's eyes like a gathering storm. "Remember batting practice?" Jon asked.

Chase's shoulders dropped like a whipped puppy putting its tail between its legs. "Yeah," Chase said. "Yeah." He shifted his eyes away from Jon. "I remember." And he did. It was the day he learned the hard way not to fuck with Jon.

"Come on, Dup. We need you," Jon said. "We will go out there and look around. If we don't find anything, we will leave and just go to the police with what we have."

Everyone in the room relaxed at Jon's statement.

"I'm in, Jon," Matt said. He got up and stood next to Chase, resting a reassuring hand on his shoulder. "Come on, Dup. You know Jon's right."

"Jon is right, Dup," Bill said. " It's the only way."

Chase licked his lips before he spoke. "Okay. Okay. I'll go."

Bill put Chase in a headlock and ruffled his hair. "That's my Dup. What a good Dup."

Chase laughed, breaking away from Bill's hold.

"Hold on, guys. We gotta think some things through." Terry stood to his feet and started to pace.

"Like what?" Bill asked.

"First, we gotta sneak out without getting caught. Second, Frenchtown Road is not just around the corner from Jon's house. It's gonna be a trek. We need to make sure we have food and water. Also, we need weapons in case we have to defend ourselves against some of those weirdos."

"Terry's right," Jon said. "What time is it, Bill?"

Bill glanced at his watch. "Ten," he said.

"Crap. Still early." Jon scratched his forehead. "Okay, here's what we'll do. First, we'll go downstairs and grab food and make water bottles. Not a lot. Just enough to hold us. We gotta travel light. We'll bring our backpacks down and put the food in them." Jon's eyes darted around the room, landing on his dresser. "Oh, and I have flashlights up here."

Jon grabbed some flashlights out of the top drawer of his dresser and tossed them to his friends. They caught them one by one, flicking them on and off to make sure they worked.

"Now, it's going to take us a good hour to bike that far. And we have to be careful," Jon said. "If we get caught, we'll be in deep shit. Sullivan Road and Greenwell Springs Road are dark at night, but we won't be in the clear till we get to Frenchtown. We'll have to stay on the edge of the roads, in the grass near the tree line."

"What about weapons?" Bill asked.

Jon twirled his flashlight in his hand a few times, then slapped it in his palm. " For weapons," he said, "we'll grab some machetes and hatchets out of the garage. We'll wait till midnight to start gathering things. My parents should be asleep by then."

"Sounds good," Bill said. He was calm and ready to go. Bill was all in and not going to back down. He was ready to die by his friends' sides.

Chase would always argue at first, putting up a big fight about everything. But eventually, he would follow Jon and Bill, so it was no surprise to Jon that he had finally bought into the plan. Chase was nervous and afraid, but committed.

"Come here," Jon said.

"Huh?" Chase rubbed his head.

"Come here. Huddle up." Jon winked at Bill.

Bill laughed, an expression of remembrance lighting up his face. "Just like the old days?"

"Yeah," Jon said. "Just like the old days."

Before Jon shot up and leaned out, he used to play center on the pee wee football team. He still remembered raising his hands and yelling, "Huddle," his voice complete with adolescent cracking.

All the boys gathered around Jon. They formed a huddle, draping their arms across one another's necks and shoulders. They stared deep into each other's eyes. Their hot breath filled the center of the huddle, mixed with smells of sodas, snack cakes, and chips.

"I know this is some scary shit," Jon said. "But this is bigger than us. We have a chance to uncover once and for all the mysteries behind Frenchtown Road."

The boys agreed with head movements.

"We are a team," Jon continued. "Best friends. And we will not, and I repeat will not split up out there."

"Good," Chase said. "Don't want to become a horror movie trope."

The boys laughed.

"No, we don't," Jon said.

"Jon?" Terry asked.

"What?"

"You sure we don't need a gun?"

The boys exchanged uncertain glances, then looked at Jon.

"No, I'm not sure," Jon said. "But I don't know how I would sneak into my parents' room and get one."

"Think you could try?" Chase asked.

"Yeah, I would feel better if we had a gun," Bill said.

John sighed. "Okay, I will try."

"Good deal," Terry said.

"One more thing," Jon said.

The boys studied Jon with anxious stares.

"No matter what happens, we will not leave each

other behind," Jon said.

"Agreed," Bill said.

"I'm all in," Chase said.

"In it until the end," Terry said.

"Behind y'all all the way," Matt said.

Jon broke the huddle. "Good. Let's relax until it's time to go."

The boys separated and sat back on the floor.

Jon turned off the television before he planted his butt on the floor. "I'm not really in the mood to watch a horror movie."

"Understood," Bill said. "I mean, considering what we saw and what we are about to do, I don't want to either."

Jon went and sprawled out on his bed on the other side of the L-shaped room, away from everyone. He needed time by himself to settle his frazzled nerves. He lay on his stomach, pillow under his chin, and stared up at the Wolverine poster on his wall. His mind raced with the myriad of scenarios and possibilities of what might be out there waiting on them. Would they run into anyone out there? The cult? The witch? Would they see mutilated cats or cattle? New satanic graffiti painted in places? But the question Jon's mind kept going back to was this: Will we have to kill anyone? He prayed to God things wouldn't go that far. If it did, would he be able to do it? Would it be like when he had gotten into fights before? Just instinct and reaction? Or would he hesitate? He didn't know, and that bothered the hell out of him.

For the next hour and a half, the boys sat in nervous silence. Chase flipped through some baseball cards Jon picked up at The Wax Pack the day before. Bill turned on the Nintendo and played Castlevania. The Punisher #34 had just been released and sat on Jon's desk, untouched; Terry picked it up and started reading. Matt pulled Cycle of the Werewolf from the bookshelf in the corner and immersed himself in it.

Midnight rolled around, and Jon set things in motion. He hopped off his bed and walked to the other section of his room. "All right, fellas, we gotta get movin'. Get your butts in gear."

The boys' bodies contorted, twitching at the sound of Jon's voice. Chase tossed the baseball cards on the ground, Terry set down his comic, and Matt closed his book. Bill was the only one who didn't respond.

"Bill," Terry said, tapping him on the shoulder.

"Hmm?" Bill still stared at the television, playing the Nintendo.

"It's time, man."

Bill breathed in deep, his chest expanding, and exhaled. "Okay." He dropped the remote and reached to power off the Nintendo.

The boys grabbed their backpacks and gathered around Jon, who now stood in front of his bedroom door.

"Listen," Jon said and looked at Chase. "And this goes especially for you."

"What?" Chase asked.

"We have to be extremely quiet going down the stairs," Jon said. "So, don't do anything stupid."

The boys nodded.

"I swear," Chase said.

"Good," Jon said. "Let's go."

Jon opened his bedroom door, and the boys snuck down the set of stairs leading to the living room. About halfway down, Jon saw his mother asleep on the couch. He turned toward his friends with his finger pressed against his lips.

"Shhhhhh," he whispered.

The five boys took careful, cat-like steps down the carpeted stairs.

The light from the television in the living room flickered. An old Western was on. Jon watched as the cowboy drew his gun and blew away a few bandits. He glanced over at his mom. Her mouth was open, and she snored, making clicking sounds.

They traveled down the stairs without incident and took a right into the kitchen. The boys eased over to the pantry on tip-toe. As they did, a sputtering noise followed by a clapping sound powered through the kitchen.

Chase farted.

Another loud smack rang out as Bill slapped Chase in the back of the head. The red in Jon's face rose like a thermometer. He wanted to strangle the two dumbasses and ram their heads together until their eyes fell out.

"Jon, what are you boys doing?" Mrs. Benson called, still half asleep.

Jon gave Bill and Chase a look from hell. "Stupid fuckers," he said. "I ought to rip your nuts off." Jon eased to the doorway and stepped into the living room. "Nothing, Mamma. Just hungry."

"Oh, okay. Listen, I'm going to bed. See y'all tomorrow." With that, she got up from the couch, turned the television off, and wobbled to the bedroom.

"Okay. Goodnight, Mamma." Jon stepped back into the kitchen.

"Whew, that was close," Terry said under a sigh.

"Yeah, no thanks to Bill and Ted here. What the hell is wrong with you, Dup?" Jon waited for an answer.

"I thought it would be silent. It felt like it was gonna be a quiet one," Chase said.

"Shit for brains," Bill said.

"You're just as stupid," Jon said to Bill.

"Listen, guys. Let's stay focused." Terry yanked the back of Jon's shirt.

"Right," Jon said, flinging Terry's hand off him.

Jon flipped on the light and walked to the pantry, his friends close behind. The boys grabbed some snacks, filled their water bottles, and stuffed them in their bags. Jon inspected his gatherings. Satisfied, he headed towards the back door.

"What about the gun?" Terry said.

Jon glanced over his shoulder. "What about it? I can't get it now, thanks to Dup and Bill."

Terry rolled his eyes. "What if we just wait a little bit? Get our other stuff, then you can come back in and get it out of your parents' room?"

"We'll see," Jon said, then opened the back door.

With the stealth of masked bandits, the boys slipped outside. They were met with the humid air of the summer night, the chirping of crickets, and the croaking of frogs.

They went to the garage and rummaged around for a few minutes. Jon grabbed three machetes, a hatchet, and a hand-held sickle. He took the hatchet and gave the machetes to Bill, Chase, and Terry. He gave the sickle to Matt.

Matt held the handle with a disapproving look. "What the hell is this?" he asked "Children of the Corn?"

"Just shut up and take it," Jon said.

Matt shrugged and stuck it in his backpack, blade facing down. The boys left the garage and walked under the patio. Moths fluttered around the yellow fluorescent light, one of them getting caught in a lone spider web.

"What do we do now?" Terry asked.

"Bill," Jon said. "How long has it been since ass blaster Chase sounded off?"

Bill glanced at his watch. "Ten minutes."

"You think your parents are sound enough

asleep?" Terry asked Jon.

"Maybe," Jon said. "I'm gonna go try."

"Okay," Terry said.

Jon walked to the back door, went inside, and shut the door behind him.

The boys stared at the empty space where Jon once stood, praying to God he would be able to get the gun.

"You think he is gonna get caught?" Matt asked.

"I don't know." Bill shrugged. "We've never done anything like this before."

"How long do you think we should give him?" Terry asked.

"Till he comes out with the gun or his mom sticks her head out the door and yells at us to come back inside," Bill said.

The boys waited in the stillness of the night, listening to the nocturnal animals sing their songs. The seconds passed as slowly as when they were in seventh period on the last day of school. An eternity later, the back door opened. They listened to the footsteps getting closer. A shadow approached.

"Jon?" Chase asked.

Jon appeared from around the corner, holding a single shot break-action .410 shotgun in his hands. The boys gave an exaggerated exhale.

Chase looked at the gun, blinking his eyes rapidly. "What the hell are you gonna do with that? Shoot squirrels?"

"Kiss my ass, Dup. It was all I had time to grab," Jon said. "My dad started to wake up."

"It's better than nothing," Terry said. "And it could still kill somebody."

The boys faced Terry, their eyes eating a hole through his face.

"I mean, not that we're gonna have to," Terry said, looking away.

"Yeah," Jon said. "It will get the job done. Now, let's go." Get the job done? Yeah, if any one of them had the balls to pull the trigger.

The boys hopped on their bikes and got their gear adjusted. They pedaled down Jon's long driveway, no one saying a word. The silence said enough. The decision had already been made, and there was no turning back. For the next hour or so, they rode their bikes from Sullivan Road all the way to the end of Frenchtown Road.

6

The boys stopped their bikes about ten yards from the trestle. The ominous structure leered down at them. Bill pointed his flashlight at it. The bridge looked like it did on the tape. The bolts in the wood seemed to be watching them, studying them, like some satanic eye hungry for their flesh. The tracks atop were rusted from years of exposure to the weather, and there were gravel-coated embankments on each side. The beams were covered in satanic graffiti of multiple colors— red, black, blue, green—sigils of Baphomet, upside down crosses, brimstone crosses, and black suns. Spray painted in blue across the top plank, just underneath the tracks, was the phrase Welcome To The Gates Of Hell.

A frigid chill permeated the atmosphere around the bridge. All the boys felt it. It was odd, uncharacteristically cold for summer, and the ambiance was heavy and oppressive. Ropes tied in miniature nooses hung from the beams underneath the trestle. Terry shined his light on them. The ropes swung with the breeze, their bottoms stained in blood.

"Fuck me," Bill said.

Jon positioned his bike, placing his feet on the ground. "What?"

"Look," Bill said, motioning with his head towards what his light revealed. "Guess that shit with the cats was real."

Jon gazed at the blood stains through the beam of light. "Of course it was real." He furrowed his brow. "All of it was real." Jon looked over his shoulder at the road. It was surrounded by a dense forest on both sides. The blanketing darkness of the night made it feel as if the woods were closing in around them. He faced the bridge again, taking in the claustrophobic scenery and inspected the writings and symbols on the old boards. He glanced left, then right, noticing the scent of the dusty gravel mixed with the pine smell of the forest. The dreaded emotion of uneasiness resurrected its claws and dug deep into Jon's soul. And it wouldn't let go.

All eyes were fixated on the demonic monument before them. It was exactly what it was labeled as: The Gates of Hell. The entrance into oblivion or a portal leading to eternal damnation. Whatever it was, it wasn't just a trestle. Not to the boys. It was a hefty, heaping dose of unbridled reality staring right back at them. It seemed to mock them, daring them to enter, saying, "Fuck around and find out, kids."

Jon was the first to break his sight away from the bridge. His eyes made the rounds to each of the boys.

Bill's arms were covered in goosebumps. Studying the symbols made his skin crawl. He looked down, rubbing his arms, making sure there wasn't something wiggling under his skin. Chase shook his head in slow, steady motions. Terry did his usual—wrinkled his nose and pushed his glasses up. He went to say something and glanced over at his brother.

Matt stared at the trestle with wild enchantment, as if the bridge drew his entire being into its sinister world.

Terry noticed the crooked smile on his brother's face. "Matt,' he said. "What is wrong with you?"

"Huh?" Matt said, looking away from the structure. "Nothing. This is just kind of …"

"Surreal," Jon said.

Jon looked at his friends again. Everyone was on edge. The bridge, the woods, what Cory told them, everything they watched on the tapes became a reality for them. "All right," he said. "Let's move closer." He lifted his legs and pedaled forward.

Bill started to follow, then he noticed Chase and Terry engrossed in observing Matt. Matt grinned from ear to ear like this was some sort of comedy show.

"Matt," Bill said. "What the hell is so funny!"

"Huh?" Matt blinked his eyes a few times, then stared back at his friends. They all had bewildered expressions on their faces. "What?" Matt asked.

"You were just sitting there grinning at the damn thing," Chase said.

"Yeah, I fail to see humor in any of this," Terry said. He saw Jon riding ahead of them. "We better catch up with Jon." Terry pedaled forward.

"What is up with your brother?" Bill asked Terry as they caught up with Jon.

"The fuck if I know," Terry said.

"Weird," Chase said and took off to catch up with the others.

The boys joined Jon under the bridge. They shined their lights back and forth across the bottom. More Tetromet symbols littered the beams.

"Man, this is some freaky shit," Chase said. His light paused at a symbol on the beams to his right. Water dripped from one of the mildewed bolts and onto the ground.

"No kidding," Terry said, gawking at the artwork.

"You can feel the evil here," Matt said and shined his light across a board. "I can feel it against my skin, like I just want to scrape it off." He stood motionless, mesmerized by a blue Tetromet symbol.

The boys stopped investigating the trestle and studied Matt again. He was creeping them the hell out.

"What the fuck is wrong with Matt?" Chase whispered.

"Nothing," Jon said. "He's right." Even in the dark, Jon saw the expressions on all their faces.

"You're right, Matt. I feel it too," Jon said. He shined the light in Matt's face, breaking him out of his daze. Matt squinted and turned away. "Come on, Matt, let's keep going."

The boys walked their bikes out from under the bridge to the other side.

"What do we do now, Jon?" Terry asked.

Jon shined his light in the tree line, examining the area. The road narrowed and the woods grew dense up ahead. "Let's put our bikes just behind the trees there. We'll go on foot the rest of the way."

The five boys dismounted their bikes and walked. Their footsteps were heavy, weighted with fear. The rubbing of the asphalt under their sneakers was a disjointed sound, as if each of them trod a path of no return. They tucked their bikes just behind the trees on the side of the road and positioned branches to give them cover. Then Jon ran up the side of the embankment and on top of the railroad tracks.

"Dude, what are you doing?" Bill asked.

"Looking for clues," Jon said. He shined his light on the trestle as he walked along the tracks. He paused. "Holy shit, guys. Get up here!" He motioned with his arm. 'Now!"

The boys took off in a sprint at the sound of Jon's beckoning. They ran up the side of the embankment with Bill in the lead. Jon was hunched over and staring at the railroad ties. His friends approached with cautious steps from behind.

"What is it, Jon?" Bill asked, squatting beside his friend.

"Blood," Jon said, holding up his hand. His fingers were covered in a red film, and the smell of blood and rusted train tracks filled the air.

"Bullshit," Chase said, pushing aside Terry and Matt to get a glimpse

Jon wiped his hand on his pants. The blood left a crimson streak on the top of his thigh.

"Oh shit, it is blood," Chase said.

"Look." Jon pointed his light at the tracks. "There's more." Fresh blood glistened like rubies in the light. It covered the ties and gravel for about five feet down the tracks.

Terry's stomach twisted in knots. His mouth watered and there was a tickle in the back of his throat. "This isn't good, fellas. I think we need to get the hell out of here. Go to the police." Terry backed away from the group, his fear becoming contagious.

The color in Chase's face had taken a hiatus long ago. He had to step away and take deep breaths at the sight of all the blood. "I think … I think Terry's right."

"Me too," Bill said, standing up. He joined Terry and Chase. "This isn't good, fellas."

Jon stood erect and faced his friends. They were now all huddled behind Matt. "You gonna join them too?" Jon asked Matt.

Matt's face made a nervous twitch, and he shrugged. "I mean, Jon, come on, man. The tapes. The blood on the tracks. That's enough to make the cops at least look into it?"

Jon wagged his head in disbelief. "I can't believe y'all," he said. "Especially you, Matt." Jon stepped forward, getting nose to nose with Matt. "One minute you are gaga and smiling over it, and the next you are ready to go home."

Matt glanced away, ashamed. Jon peeked over Matt's shoulder and addressed Bill, Terry, and Chase.

"You know what?" Jon asked. "I bet they are out there in the woods watching us now." He pointed at the forest, then behind him at the blood. "I bet as soon as we leave, they are gonna come out and clean all this shit up. Then, when we get back with the cops, it will all be gone, and we are gonna be left with our thumbs up our ass. The cops will just chalk it up as the overactive imagination of some fucking punk kids trying to play off people's tragedy! Or trying to get famous for busting this shit wide open again! Don't you get it?" Jon held out both arms.

"Get what, Jon?" Bill yelled. "That this is some real fucked up and scary shit that we have no business being involved in? Yeah, we get it!"

"No," Jon said. He eased around Matt and walked over to Bill. "That this is just what Craddock and those sick fucks want."

"Oh yeah? And what exactly is that?" Chase asked.

"They want us to leave and stay silent," Jon said. He spun on his heels with a quick turn, leaned into Matt's ear, and said, "That is what they want. So they can keep. On. Killing."

"Jon," Bill said. "No way they can clean all that up. It's all over the gravel, man. Plus, it will stain the ties. The police will see that. They're not complete idiots. The tape with the man getting killed by the train and the blood on the tracks … enough evidence." Bill placed a hand on Jon's shoulder. "Come on, man, let's go. We've accomplished what we came out here to do."

Jon adjusted, facing Bill. He placed his hands on his hips and looked to the side. He thought about their argument. Why didn't he want to just leave? Curiosity? Adventure? Maybe he liked the thrill of danger? He didn't know. But what he did know? His friends made sense. Maybe he shouldn't push it. After all, what were five kids against a cult of grownups? Also, maybe they had guns too. What would machetes, axes, and a break-action .410 do against that?

Just turn in the evidence and let the police deal with it, Jon thought.

"Okay," Jon said. He breathed in and exhaled. "Y'all are right. Let's go back to my house, get the tapes, and go to the police."

Sighs of relief ascended from the boys' mouths all the way into the heavens.

"Thank God," Chase said. He relaxed his shoulders and rolled his neck.

Terry placed his hands on his hips and stared up at the night sky. "No kidding."

"Good deal," Bill said and smirked at Jon. "Damn good deal." He slapped Jon on the shoulder. "Now let's go."

Matt heard his friends walk off, but he couldn't turn his gaze away from the blood. This wasn't supposed to happen. This was supposed to be fun. They were supposed to come out here and enjoy the bridge and be done. But blood? Real blood? Matt was ashamed for getting so excited about it all. This wasn't a joke, and someone was dead.

Jon stared over his shoulder at Matt. "You coming?"

"Yeah," he said and turned around. "I'm coming."

Matt joined his friends. They walked off the track and down the embankment. The five boys strolled under the bridge and, this time, didn't even glance at the symbols.

"Should we call the police right away when we get home?" Terry asked.

"I don't know," Jon said.

"Do you think we should wake your parents up and tell them about all this? Show them the tapes too," Chase said.

"I don't know, guys," Jon said. "Let's just focus on getting out of here."

They went to the trees where they hid their bikes. Matt wrestled to get his free from a branch that had wormed its way through the spokes of his front tire. Terry knocked his kickstand down, settled his bike, then went to help his brother. The two jerked on it, but the branch wouldn't give.

"How many dumbasses does it take to get a bike loose?" Chase asked.

Jon and Bill snickered. Everyone was more at ease

since they were getting the fuck out of there and going home.

"Hey, Matt, why don't you piss on it. Or better yet, get Terry to shoot his wad on it. Might need some lubrication to slip it—"

A deafening shrill from within the woods interrupted Bill's joke. It was a girl's scream. She sounded terrified or, worse, injured. It lasted for about three seconds. Terry and Matt froze mid tug, eyes expanding behind their glasses. There was a noticeable tremble in Bill's hands, shaking the handlebars on his bike. Chase had been riding in circles, and his bike came to a jarring halt. A cold shiver coiled around Jon's spine and squeezed.

The shriek filled the night air again. This time with more of a staccato rhythm.

Chase lost his shit. "Ohmygod Ohmygod they're killing her! We gotta go! We gotta go! I don't want to die out here, Jon. I wanna go home. I wanna go home! Now!"

The relaxed atmosphere was no more. An insidious dread draped over the boys and zipped closed around them like a body bag. They wanted nothing more than to be back safe in their own beds and out of this fucking forest.

The girl screamed once more.

Chase started to cry. "Come on, Jon! I wanna go!"

No one moved. They all stared at Jon, waiting for him to give orders.

The pounding in Jon's head seemed to drown out

Chase's pleas. It was like they were having a conversation underwater and all Jon could hear were hollow echoes. Bill said something and so did Terry, but Jon couldn't understand. Then, it was like his inner man came up and took a breath. Jon was a protector at his core, especially when it came to girls. Maybe because he always wanted a little sister to take care of and look out for? He didn't know, but one thing he was sure of? A coward, he was not. Jon composed himself, narrowed his brow, and said, "We can't leave her. We have to save her." He stepped off his bike.

Chase wailed, bumbling over to Jon and falling around his legs. "No, no, no. I wanna be in my own bed. I wanna go home. They're gonna kill us too, Jon!" Chase gazed up at his friend with a wet face and pleading eyes. "Chop us into pieces like on the video or tie us to a slab and gut us with a goddamn goat horn!"

Jon yanked Chase up by the collar. He wobbled as if his legs were made of rubber bands. Jon brought a clenched fist right across his jaw, knocking Chase to the ground. "Get a hold of yourself, chicken shit," Jon yelled at him.

Chase let out a muffled huff minced with sobs and rolled onto his back. He stared up at the summer moon hanging in the sky, tears and blood streaming down his face.

Jon stepped to Chase and leaned over him. "Afraid! That girl screaming her ass off out there is terrified," Jon said, pointing at the woods. "And by the sounds of her screams, I bet she's younger than we are." He stood erect, eyes still cemented on Chase.

"That poor thing needs our help, so I'm going to help her." Jon paced over to his bike, grabbed his hatchet and the .410 shotgun. He pulled a shell from his pocket, cracked the barrel, and loaded it, then whipped it shut and bolted over to his friends.

"I'd rather die than know I chickened out and let some little girl die when I could have done something to stop it," Jon said, eyes on fire. "So, go on if you wanna go home. You do, and you're an accomplice to murder." Jon placed the hatchet in his waistband and held the shotgun like a marching soldier. He reached down, grabbed Chase by the shirt, and yanked him to his feet. "Go home, pussy," Jon said, shoving Chase away.

Chase regained his balance, his lip puffy and bleeding. He wiped his mouth with the back of his hand and stared at the blood. "Blood," he said.

"Yeah, no shit," Jon said.

Chase's chest expanded with each deep breath. "You're right, Jon. We can't let her end up being splattered all over the tracks like the others."

"We gotta help her," Bill said. "We can't leave her."

Chase wiped his mouth with the bottom of his shirt, then spat. He bent over, placing his hands on his knees. He cocked his head up, all the resistance gone from his eyes.

Jon unclenched his fist, his body relaxing. "Sorry I punched you," he said. "But you were losing it."

Chase shook his head and waved at Jon. "Don't

apologize," he said.

Jon lifted his head to the summer sky and twinkling stars. "Come on, guys," he said. "Grab your shit and let's go."

The boys obeyed. They gathered at the edge of the woods, weapons in hands and flashlights lit.

Jon stepped into the dark morass of the forest first. His light illuminated the bristling weeds and curling branches, casting imp like shadows with every movement. "Listen, guys," he said. "Remember what we agreed to. We do not split up. Do you hear me? We stay together no matter what. That's how we survive."

The boys stared at the edge of the trees, surveying the forest. They listened as the sound of chirping crickets and croaking frogs sang their nocturnal songs. Jon's light made crisscross patterns, illuminating sections of twisted branches and leaves. They entered the woods and stood next to Jon.

The claustrophobic oppression was immediate. One moment they were standing on an open road, the next, they were transported into the belly of the beast. Unknown shadows whirled around them, and every movement sent surges of fresh terror through their hearts. It was the type of fear that made a person question everything. The movement of the trees—was it the wind shaking a branch, or a red hooded cult member coming to spill their blood?

"Which direction?" Bill asked. He stopped and shined his light, then turned in circles.

"It sounded like it came from that way," Terry

said, and pointed his flashlight to their left. "Back deep."

"I think Terry's right," Jon said. He changed directions and headed deep into the heart of the woods.

The boys walked, flashlights darting in every direction, searching every sound and exposing all the shadows. There was no conversation, only the sound of heavy breathing and snapping limbs. The boys entered deeper into the wooded abyss.

A scream filled the night air again. This time, it was closer.

Jon's heart tried to crawl up his chest. He pointed his light at a massive oak tree in the distance. "That sounded close. Around that tree. Less than fifty yards away," he said. "Come on."

The boys shifted gears into a dead sprint. Their feet crunched branches and leaves while their flashlights cut through the forest like lightning. They arrived at the tree, and as they came under the cover of its branches, the girl screamed again. She sounded about twenty yards ahead.

"Hey, come here," Jon said. He motioned for the boys to circle up around him and whispered, "Turn off your lights."

The boys fumbled with their lights and shut them off.

"Listen, she's close," Jon said. "That means they are as well. We keep the lights off so we don't give away our position. We walk in a line, holding hands. That's how we stay together."

Everything was pitch black, and the five friends waited for their eyes to adjust. They stood motionless, and another high-pitched screech belted across the woods.

"Shit," Matt said.

"The fuck," Bill said.

The screech came from the trees behind them.

"What is that? It sounds different than the one we heard near the bridge," Chase said.

The noise came again.

"What is that?" Chase said again.

"Shhhh," Jon said. "It's just a screech owl."

"How the hell do you know?" Bill asked.

"Because I know," Jon said. "I live in the woods, remember."

"I ain't taking another step till we shine a light up there and see," Chase said.

"I said no more light," Jon said.

"And I said I ain't taking another step till you let me see the damn owl," Chase said.

"Shit, now is not the time. We need to find the girl," Jon said.

"Jon, just turn on the light and be done with it," Bill said.

"Fine, pussies." Jon turned on his torch and pointed it up at the branches of the tree. He waved it around until a pair of eyes glowed back at them. The owl screeched.

"See," Jon said. "Now, can we go?" He shined his light in Chase's face. "You satisfied?"

"Yes," Chase said.

"Good." Jon turned off his light.

The boys put their weapons in their backpacks and flashlights in their waistbands. Jon pulled the butt of the gun tight against his shoulder. "Y'all hold hands," Jon said. "I will stay in front."

The boys held hands and proceeded to walk in the direction of the girl's scream, with Jon ahead of them. They made it a few feet past the trunk of the oak tree when something rustled in the woods to their right.

"What was that?" Chase whispered.

"Shut up and keep moving," Jon instructed. He turned to the direction of the noise.

More rustling. This time, behind them.

"There it is again," Bill said, his voice escalating.

"And don't you tell me that is a fucking owl, Jon," Chase said.

"Shhhh," Jon said, still trying to move the group forward. He turned in circles and pointed the gun into the dark. A bead of sweat dripped into Jon's eye, and he wiped it with his shoulder. His hands shook so bad he was scared he would pull the trigger by mistake. He eased his finger off the trigger and rested it on the guard.

"Why does it matter if we are quiet? Whatever it is

knows we're here," Bill said. He pulled his hands away from Chase and Terry. He slipped off his backpack, retrieved his machete, then turned on his flashlight. Bill's hands were shaky, and it was evident by the erratic beam of the flashlight.

"What are you doing?" Jon asked.

"Like I said, whatever is out there knows we're here. And it's circling us. Listen."

The boys paused. They stood in the dark, waiting to hear the sounds. More rustling noises. This time to their left.

Jon eased his backpack to the ground and fetched his hatchet. "Bill's right. Grab your weapons. Turn on your lights!"

Jon didn't have to tell them twice. Chase, Matt, and Terry switched on their lights and grabbed their weapons as fast as their adolescent hands allowed.

This time, a real scream came from ten yards in front of them. It was behind a row of trees. The shriek banged on their eardrums.

"What the hell?" Chase closed his eyes.

Jon shined his light in the direction of the scream. "Motherfu—"

Terry joined his light with Jon's. "Oh, dear God, help us."

All the boys now shined their lights at the same spot. The creature from the tapes crouched in the trees, visible from the torso up. They could see the horns that protruded from its eye sockets and curved around the top of its head, and its leathery gray skin gleamed in the light. Saliva dripped from its opaque teeth as it opened its mouth wide and screamed.

"It's the … fucking … the tape …" Terry said. His teeth chattered, and his muscles were like lead. His bladder gave way, and the warm piss cascaded down his leg. Tunnel vision set in as his mind went haywire.

"The monster …" Chase whimpered. He stared at the demon's horns and sharp teeth. He tried to swallow, but his throat was closed off. It was hard to breathe, and his head throbbed. The creature screamed again, sending Chase into a sprint.

Chase's movement jolted Terry out of his fear induced daze, and he bolted off in a different direction.

Bill and Jon's flashlights stayed on the demon. It took another step forward, illuminating more of its body. Matt stood stoic. His breathing was labored, and his glasses fogged. The demon eased closer to Matt as it came out from behind the trees. Matt's muscles broke free from their concrete tomb, and he darted off into the heart of the forest.

Bill dropped his flashlight to the ground. "Holy fucking hell."

Jon stood steady, his light frozen on the creature's face.

Bill tried to speak again. He struggled to get it out, but when he did, there was no mistaking what he said.

"It's from the tape!" Bill got his ass in motion and darted off into the dark.

Jon couldn't move—couldn't run, couldn't walk,

couldn't even twitch his pinkie finger. He stood intoxicated by this ... thing. This creature from the tapes, the same monster Cory had seen years ago. The creature eased away from the trees and changed direction towards Jon. Jon's muscles finally obeyed his brain, and he eased the light down. He saw long fingers with black knife-like fingernails extended from its hands. He watched as its muscles rippled with each breath, its arms swaying back and forth as it walked like some demonic primate. He listened as the creature's cloven hooves crept towards him, snapping branches with each step.

The beam from Jon's light bobbled as he snugged the butt of the gun against his shoulder. "Get back or I will blow a fucking hole in you!"

The demon continued towards him.

Jon pulled the trigger on the shotgun, and a loud boom echoed through the woods. The pellets from the blast hit it right in the chest, and a geyser of black liquid exploded from the wound. The leather skin of the creature was mangled and bleeding, but it seemed to be unaffected by the blast. The demon jutted its head forward, screaming in anger. Jon flinched, dropping the gun. That was all the time the beast needed.

Before Jon could blink, the creature left its feet and was on top of him. There was a burning pain in his shoulders as black fingernails punctured flesh. Jon winced, letting go of his flashlight. The monster wrestled him to the ground, straddling him and digging its fingernails deeper into his shoulders. The creature got nose to nose with Jon, then puffed its hot breath into his face. Jon coughed and gagged.

The smell, he thought. That smell … it smells like …

The grooved horns. The leathery skin. The demon's blood soaking through his shirt. He stared at the thing's teeth and placed the familiar aroma of its breath.

Oh. My. God, Jon thought with horror. Smells like whiskey and shit … Craddock! This fucking thing is Craddock!

"Help me!" Jon screamed. "Bill! Dup! Terry! Matt! It is Craddock! This fucking thing is Craddock!"

Jon bucked and kicked like a wild stallion. The creature stayed in position, wrenching its claws deeper into Jon. He heard one more deafening scream before everything faded to black.

7

Jon awoke on the forest floor. Darkness still blanketed the sky, so he figured he couldn't have been out for too long. He blinked, lifting his head and examining his chest and all the way down to his feet. The creature had vanished, and he was still in the same spot on the ground. He eased up to a sitting position.

"My head," he mumbled. Jon closed his eyes and rubbed his temples. His head felt funny, like he was in a fog. He opened his eyes and stared out at the forest. Everything seemed distant, as if he viewed it all from afar. He moved a hand to his shoulder. The punctures from the creature's fingernails were gone.

Did I imagine it? he thought. No. Can't be. We all saw it. I shot it. Jon placed a hand on the ground and rose to one knee. His head twirled as if his mind were caught on a merry-go-round.

"Bill! Dup! Terry! Matt!" His voice sounded distant and muffled. Cold. Jon crossed his arms over his chest, rubbing the backs of them with his hands.

Numb, he thought. My fingers are numb. He saw the goosebumps on his arms but couldn't feel them on his fingertips. His senses were misfiring, leaving a metallic taste in his mouth.

There was no answer from his friends. Jon cried out again. "Bill! Dup! Terry! Matt!" He squinted and focused on his hearing, trying to discern any noise. Nothing but frogs and crickets.

He sniffed.

And smelled it.

Whiskey and shit.

His head pounded, and reality spun around him. The night's events all started to piece together in his mind. Cory. The tapes. The road. The trestle. His friends. The demon. Craddock. The smell of alcohol and feces was so strong, Jon brought his hands to his nose. "Jesus," he said, hacking.

Jon rose to his feet and took a step forward. What the hell is going on? His body was lighter. Much lighter, as if he were a mist floating through the forest.

"This is weird," he said. "Like walking in a bounce house." He took another step, then another. If he didn't know any better, he would've sworn something or someone guided him. All his extremities were weightless, and some force was having its way with him like a feather in the wind. He swung his arms, picking up his pace. He caught a glimpse of one arm out the corner of his eye. The flesh and adolescent hair had disappeared, replaced by a gray and leathery exterior. He glanced again, and this time, it was back to normal. Jon tried to make his arms stop swinging. He wanted to take a gander at what the hell he thought he saw, but his body wouldn't cooperate.

A deep sense of helplessness asphyxiated Jon's soul. Something or someone was controlling his movements. His consciousness made a push to rid himself of the weird feeling. The tunnel vision dissipated, and the grogginess faded. The sensation had only lasted a few seconds.

Hands.

Old, decrepit, wrinkly hands with yellow, infected fingernails.

They were not gripping his body, but his soul. He saw them in his mind's eye like a movie playing across the screen. With his physical eyes, he saw the forest and his gray, leathery arms. In his mind, he saw the hands gripping his arms. The supernatural hands dragged his soul back down to whatever realm it was he tried to escape. The grogginess returned, the tunnel vision kicked back in, and the total loss of control became permanent. His inner being seemed to be wrapped in chains. He struggled and fought to rise to the surface, but something or someone held him down. He felt as if he were buried alive in his own body. Jon screamed. He kicked his legs and flailed his arms. The fear was like nothing he had ever experienced before. It seemed to work its way into every square inch of his body, suffocating any hope of deliverance.

"Over there. To your right. Behind that tree."

Craddock's voice reverberated through every particle in Jon's body. Its origin was deep, right from inside the well of his heart.

A revelation came to Jon. A dark, sinister knowledge he wished he'd never discovered. Craddock had control of him … all of him. He was lodged down deep in Jon's psyche, a splinter in the skin not coming loose. Jon felt constrained in a straitjacket of darkness with no way out.

Dear God! He's inside me! Craddock … or whatever this thing is. It's inside me!

"No use fighting, boy. This is my playground now, motherfucker," Craddock's voice growled.

Jon watched, a spectator, through the lens of his eyes as his feet carried him to his right. When he saw what lay on the ground next to the tree, Jon screamed. He screamed on the inside, but no sound escaped his mouth.

Oh no! Oh dear God no! This can't happen! It can't be real! Unbridled dread and terror violated his stream of consciousness. He heard Craddock's voice again and smelled his scent.

"There they are. Just a waitin' for ya. Pick 'em up. Put it on."

Jon stood directly over the objects. He picked up the black goat head first and put it on his head. It reeked of body odor and treated leather. He grabbed the video camera next, flipping on its light and mashing RECORD. The camera hummed, and the tape went in motion. Last, he grabbed his hatchet. With the camera on his shoulder and the hatchet hanging by his side, Jon turned slowly and took a step back toward the oak tree.

He heard Craddock's voice again.

"Get 'em for me, Jonny boy. Cut 'em up and pile their pieces high. Record it all. I want to see it and see it good, boy; you understand?"

Jon heard himself speak, but it didn't sound like his voice. It was low, deep, and guttural. "How will I catch them?"

"The woods, boy, she won't let them leave."

"Who is she?"

"Theodosia, boy. She's queen out here. She's settled over this place like the mornin' fog. Doin' the Tetromet's will."

Jon meandered through the forest, stepping over logs and tearing through thorn bushes. He came to a clearing with a solitary tree.

Matt stood next to it with an emotionless stare, gazing at the trunk. His glasses were gone, and sweat mixed with blood ran down his face. He placed both hands on the trunk, swayed, and started to tap his head on the trunk, mumbling, "Can't ... get ... out ... can't ... go ... home ... she's here ... she lives here ... I saw his tree ... I saw his tree ... I saw his tree ..."

With each sway, Jon saw who controlled Matt. Whenever Matt's head would tap the tree, her face came into view. She stood beside him, wearing a black dress. Her frayed white hair was fixed in a ponytail atop her head. Empty, black eye sockets stared back at him, and the Tetromet symbol was carved into her forehead. The skin and muscle on her jaw had rotted off, leaving behind dingy bones and a mouth of missing teeth.

Jon wanted to yell at Matt, to tell him to run, but he knew Matt wouldn't hear him.

Jon watched through the lens of the camera and hoisted the hatchet above his head. He sank it into the back of Matt's skull. Matt's body twitched, then toppled to the ground. Jon bent over and removed the hatchet from Matt's head. Blood poured from the wound, soaking the leaves and twigs.

Jon glanced to his left. Theodosia stood there, her back to him. She floated away to her next victim, motioning with her finger for Jon to follow.

The last thing Jon remembered before the darkness swallowed him was the snapping of Matt's bones as he hacked him to pieces. He blacked out to Craddock's voice.

"Record it, boy. Record it all."

8

Terry sat behind a rotten stump, his head resting between his legs. He rocked back and forth, crying, "Go away. Please, God, make her go away." His glasses were on the ground next to him, and snot hung from his nose in long, translucent strings. Perspiration dripped into his eyes, and he gave rapid blinks. He didn't want to look up. He knew she was still there. He smelled her. It was a sour aroma mixed with shit and old people smell. It reminded Terry of the time he visited his grandfather in a nursing home two years before, before he died. And that was the other smell he identified. Death. It had a lingering, foreboding smell, sour and full of rot.

Where are my friends? Where is my brother? Terry thought. Are they okay? Are they dead? I heard Matt scream! Oh dammit! Matt! Dear Jesus, please let him be okay. Please! Please! Please! I just want to go home. I want this to be over. Why did I let Jon talk us into this?

"Terry," a voice said.

No, Terry thought. It can't be.

Terry lifted his head and opened his eyes. "Matt?"

"Yeah, it's me," Matt said.

It was Matt. Standing right in front of him. Terry grabbed his flashlight, flipped it on, and shined it at his brother. Sweat beaded across Matt's face, and his blond hair was plastered to his forehead.

"It really is you," Terry said. "But I heard you scream. I thought you were dead." He picked his glasses up off the ground and put them back on.

"No," Matt said, shaking his head. "I was just really scared."

Terry examined his surroundings. Nothing but darkness and swaying branches. "Where did she go?" he asked. "She was just here a few moments ago."

"Who?" Matt asked.

"The old lady in the black dress. She said her name was Theodosia."

"I don't know," Matt said, shrugging his shoulders. "I heard you crying. That's how I found you."

"I don't know then," Terry said. "But we better go before she comes back."

Matt helped Terry off the ground. "I think I know the way out. Come on." Matt turned and started to walk away. "Let's get out of here."

"What about Jon, Bill, and Dup?" Terry asked.

"I don't know." Matt glanced over his shoulder at Terry. "I've been walking around for a long time. I haven't seen them or heard them."

"What about that monster? You seen it?"

"No, nothing. Now come on, let's go. The sooner we call the cops, the better."

Terry followed his brother through the forest. The mosquitos swarmed, buzzing in their ears and biting their necks. Then there were the thorns relentlessly tearing and ripping at their flesh and clothes, appearing as if out of nowhere.

They made it to a clearing, and Terry saw a light coming towards them.

"Matt, you see that light?" Terry asked and pointed.

"Yeah, I do. I wonder if it's Bill."

"I don't know, but it's coming fast." Terry cupped his hands around his mouth. "Bill! Is that you?"

No answer.

"Dup? Jon?" Terry called again.

Then the light went out.

"Shit," Terry said. "Where did it go?"

"Hell if I know," Matt said and placed his finger over his mouth. "Shhh, listen."

The brothers listened for rustling leaves or cracking branches, anything indicating movement. All they heard was the buzzing of the mosquitos and the sound of their own breathing.

"Fuck, Terry, what is that?" Matt pointed at a tree about fifteen yards away.

"What? I don't see anything!"

"Over there, by that tree. It looks like an outline of a person," Matt said.

Terry squinted. Chills arose all over his body, and his ears burned. "What the hell is that?"

"I don't know. Shine your light. I lost mine," Matt said.

"Okay, move out of the way." Terry stepped in front of Matt. He turned on his flashlight and put the beam on the figure. "Holy motherfucking shit! The creature!"

The demon stood with its mouth agape, taking heavy breaths. One arm swayed at its side, and the other held a video camera. The demon pointed it right at them.

"Jesus fucking Christ," Terry gasped. "Matt, we gotta get out of here." Terry turned and faced his brother.

And screamed.

And screamed.

And screamed.

Matt was no more. Staring back at him was Theodosia.

"You will make an excellent addition to our tree, young one," Theodosia said.

Terry couldn't move. He couldn't speak. All he

could do was scream.

Jon Benson was still unconscious. Edgar Craddock had total control of his demon body. The goat skull and Jon's head had fused together, becoming one. Craddock turned the camera back on and started to record. Through the lens, he saw the back of Terry's head. He walked over with the hatchet hoisted over his head, the blunt side ready to strike.

Terry didn't notice the demon behind him. He was too terrified by Theodosia. There was a loud crack as the demon brought the back side of the hatchet down on Terry's skull. Terry's knees buckled, and he toppled to the ground and onto his back. The demon stepped over Terry and straddled him with the camera in one hand and the hatchet in the other.

The demon filmed as it brought the hatchet down. There was a loud crunch as the blow caved the bridge of Terry's nose into his face. His glasses broke in half, and blood pumped from the crater in his face. Over and over again, the demon hammered on Terry's face and skull. The camera picked up every sound of the thudding weapon and the cracking bones.

The demon pounded away until Terry's face was an unrecognizable stew of blood, bones, and flesh, his head dented in like a crushed soda can. On the last blow, the handle of the hatchet broke. The demon paused, gripping the handle. It cocked its head towards Theodosia and screeched, then hit pause on the camera and stood up.

"I will go get the others," Theodosia said. She

turned and disappeared into the darkness of the forest.

Jon Benson regained consciousness. It was like waking up from a vivid dream. He struggled to shake the grogginess. Everything was still distant, and he felt weightless. Jon looked around. Nothing had changed since the last time he was conscious—it was dark, and he was in the woods. He tried to speak, but the words were inside his own head.

"Bill! Dup! Terry!"

Then he remembered Matt.

"Oh God! Matt! Matt! What did I do! What did I do! Fuck! Fuckfuckfuck!"

"I see someone is awake," Craddock said.

"What did you do?" Jon asked.

"Hell, boy, I didn't do shit. You did."

Jon felt his body walking. Something turned his head, and he saw his arms and feet—gray, leathery, and with claws.

"What the fuck did you do to me, Craddock? Why do I look like this!? Why don't I have control over my own body?" Jon asked.

"Ain't your body no more, boy. It's mine," Craddock said. "You boys should have left well enough alone. Now, all your friends are gonna die. Fuck 'em up. One, two, three."

"What the hell are you?" Jon asked. He cried, but there were no tears.

"I'm a high-ranking demon guardian for the Tetromet, and you will soon be one as well. Not as powerful as me, but a guardian nonetheless. It will only take a few more days for your soul to bond with your new body and your final transformation will be complete. But until then, I'm gonna be here with you, boy, making sure you don't do no stupid shit. So, like I said. It's my body now, motherfucker."

"You can't do this," Jon said.

"But I am, you little cock-sucking shit stain. Now, sit your ass back and watch 'cause you're about to kill Chase."

Chase had climbed a tree. He sat on one of the branches with his back leaned against the trunk. He hadn't heard the slightest movement in hours. He had walked and walked but couldn't find his way out of the forest, so he'd scrambled up a tree to wait until dawn.

Please be okay, fellas, Chase thought. God, please keep them safe. Please let us make it out of here. Chase prayed as he listened to the chirping crickets and swatted mosquitoes away from his face.

"Chase! Chase Dupuy! Where are you?" a man's voice called.

What the hell, Chase thought.

"Chase! Chase Dupuy! This is Sargent Belk from the Central Police Department," the man said.

Oh thank God, Chase thought. He didn't notice the Sargent wasn't shining a flashlight.

"I'm up here," Chase shouted. "In the tree! Can you hear me?"

"Yeah," Belk said. "I hear you. I'm right below you."

Chase adjusted and gazed down at the ground. The shadowy outline of man stood there next to the tree. Chase pulled out his flashlight and shined it on him. Relief ran over him in waves. It was an officer.

"Look, we got Jon, Bill, Matt, and Terry down at the Central Police Station," Belk said.

"Are they all okay?" Chase asked. He crossed his fingers, closed his eyes, and pursed his lips. Please say yes, please say yes, please say yes.

"Yeah," Belk said. "They are fine."

Chase relaxed his face and uncrossed his fingers. "Thank God," he sighed.

"What was that?" Belk asked.

"Nothing. I'm coming down."

Chase scurried down the tree and stood on the ground next to Belk. Belk was an average height and, from what Chase could see in the dark, had red hair and a red beard. Static crackled from the walkie on the shoulder of his blue uniform.

Belk placed a hand on Chase's shoulder. "Look, I know you and your friends have been through hell. They told us about the tapes and the blood. We have the tapes as evidence, and my crew is gathering samples of the blood. It was a dumb thing you kids did. Brave, but stupid. Hopefully, we can find out who is

EZEKIEL KINCAID | 157

behind this."

Chase nodded. "Can we leave? I want to see my friends and go home."

"Absolutely. Your mom has been notified, and she is at the station with your friends, waiting on you," Belk said. He reached over and pushed a button on his walkie. "This is Belk. I've got the boy. We're headed back."

"Good. Let's get out of here."

Belk and Chase traveled through the woods. Chase shined his light, still not noticing Belk was without a flashlight.

"Stop," Belk said, grabbing Chase by the shoulder. "Turn off the light, quick."

"Wha—why?"

"Shhhh," Belk whispered. "Just do it."

Chase turned off his torch.

"Look," Belk said. "Beyond the trees, just up ahead. A light."

Chase saw it. "Shit. It's them. It's gotta be them."

The light approached, expanding and pulsating.

Fifty yards.

Forty.

Thirty.

Twenty.

Then it shut off.

"Where did it go?" Chase whispered.

"Shhh," Belk said.

Chase heard the crunching of leaves and snapping of branches. Something was running towards them.

Then a flash of light blinded Chase, and something tackled him to the ground.

"Officer Belk! Officer Belk! Help!" Chase screamed.

Chase could feel the suffocating weight of a body on top of him. The blinding light was still in his face, so he turned his head away and stared out into the forest. Splotches of colors filled his vision.

"Officer Belk! Where are you?" Chase yelled again. His vision returned. Standing about five feet away from his head was an old lady. Gray, wiry hair snaked down her head, and she wore a black dress. He recognized her from the tapes.

"Oh my God it's—"

"Theodosia," she said in officer Belk's voice.

"Fuckohfuckohfuck!" Panic coiled around Chase's insides like a python.

This was just the beginning of the terror.

Chase turned his head to see who or what was on his chest. His eyes bulged, and he opened his mouth so wide the skin connecting his mouth and cheeks threatened to rip. The creature they saw earlier in the forest sat on his chest, filming him with a camcorder.

"Fuuuuuuuck!   Oh   God!   Fuuuuuuck!

Shitohshitohshit! Help me! God!" Chase tried to fight it off.

The demon made a fist and punched Chase in the throat.

Chase gasped for air, lifting his head up and down.

Jon watched the events unfold, terror swirling in his heart. "Craddock, you sick fuck! Let him go!"

Craddock placed the camera up to one of his horns and gave a sinister laugh. "Nah, boy. You gonna watch yourself kill your buddy."

"Dup! No! Dup!" Jon yelled.

His claws sliced across Chase's face, leaving deep lacerations. Blood splattered through the air and leaked from the gashes.

"Oh God! It burns so bad!" Chase screamed.

The demon struck again, slicing more of Chase's face open. Mangled flesh and muscle dangled from Chase's cheeks.

"Please! Please stop," Chase begged. He cried and screamed … and remembered …

He was five years old when his dad left them. He stood outside in his driveway holding He-Man in one hand and Trap Jaw in another. His dad held a suitcase and was storming to his tan 1982 Buick Regal. His mom chased after his dad in tears, pleading for him not to go. His dad threw his suitcase in the car and pushed his mom away.

"I am done with you and that little shit for good," he had said. Then he got in the car and drove off.

Chase's mom fell to the ground in anguish, weeping in their front yard. Chase had stood there in shock with his mouth open, still holding his action figures. He didn't move. He didn't go over to his mom. He just stood there, stunned.

As he was about to die, all Chase could think about was his dad. Why did he leave? His mom never told him. Why didn't he call? Or write? Or visit? All Chase ever wanted was a dad … his dad. He held out hope he would see his dad again one day. But now, on the precipice of death, the hope evaporated.

"Daddy! Daddy!" Chase bellowed. "Why? I want you! Where are you! Please, Daddy! What did I do wrong!? Why didn't you love me!? Daddy! I'm dying. All I ever wanted was to see you! To hug you! I wanted you to take me to games! Watch me play sports! Daddy!"

Jon heard his friend's heartfelt pleas. He saw Chase's tears among the blood and flesh.

"Dammit, Dup! I love you! My family loves you! My Dad loves you! Dup! Dup!" Jon yelled and wept with his friend. "Dup!"

The claw raked down Chase's face, fileting away more skin.

"Daddy! Help!" Chase screamed. "Daddy—"

Chase's cry was cut off when the demon rammed its claws down his throat.

Gurgling and gagging sounds rose from Chase as the demon removed its claw. The creature brought its hand close to the camera. It was curled into a fist, blood dripping from the knife-like fingernails and spilling out the edges.

"You sick fucking bastard," Jon yelled.

The demon opened his hand. Chase's severed tongue sat in the palm. Craddock laughed, then moved the camera back on Chase.

Chase made unintelligible sounds and coughed up blood.

"Craddock, you fucker, that is my friend! You sick shit! My friend! Do you hear me?" Jon yelled.

"Yeah, " Craddock said. "And he is about to be your dead friend." Craddock placed the camera down by the side of Chase's head.

Jon saw Chase's profile and a close up of his ear. The skin on his face looked like it had been run through a paper shredder.

"Leave him alone, Craddock!"

Jon watched as the demon placed the claw of its pointer finger next to Chase's ear. He couldn't see the other side, but he assumed Craddock was doing the same thing to it as well. With a slow, steady motion, the demon eased his claws into Chase's ears.

Chase wailed.

Craddock turned and twisted his nails, inserting his fingers farther into Chase's ears.

More screams.

"No," Jon yelled.

The demon yanked its claws towards its body, and

they came tearing out of the top of

Chase's face and nose.

"Craddock, I hate you! You bastard!" Internally, Jon screamed. Externally, his demon

body picked up the camera.

Craddock's insidious laugh made Jon sick. "One more to go, boy. One more to go. And this one is gonna be a doozy."

Bill made his way back to the spot where they first encountered the demon. He heard Chase's screams and pleas to his father. It was too much for Bill to handle. He fell to his knees and started to retch. The vomit was rank with sour soft drinks and snack cakes. Tears rolled down Bill's cheeks from the intensity of the heaves. He finished hurling, then wiped his eyes and mouth with his shirt.

"Dup," he wept. "Oh my God. He's dead ... dead." Bill buried his face in his hands, crying harder. "Jon, I hope you're okay. Jon, please don't be dead. I don't want to lose my best friend. Jon, please be alive. We gotta find Terry and Matt ... we gotta ... Dup is dead ... Oh God ..." Bill's voice intensified. He slapped his hands over his mouth, muffling his outburst. He hoped he hadn't given away his position.

The thought of the demon possibly knowing his location froze Bill's blood. He breathed in rapid, short breaths, and his heart slammed against his ribcage. His skin grew clammy, and his mind cycloned out of control. Lightheaded, he dropped to all fours and rocked his body.

"I don't wanna die," he whispered. "I don't wanna die. I don't wanna die. I don't wanna die. Please, Jesus, I don't wanna die."

Fifteen yards away, the leaves rustled.

"Oh fuck. Oh fuck," Bill wheezed. "It's the monster; he's back!" Every particle in Bill's anatomy abandoned all hope. He curled up into a ball and wept, his body quaking with grief. The cries were mixed with intermittent wheezing pleas. "I … can't … just … no … Jon … I … I …" He breathed in, smelling the scent of the forest floor and the dirt, then exhaled, his breath leaving him in quivers. He prayed while he waited to die. "Our Father, who art in heaven, hallowed be Thy name. Thy kingdom come, Thy will be—"

"Bill, it's me," a voice said.

Bill stopped praying and uncurled. He rolled on his side, opening his eyes, and said, "Jon?"

"Yeah, it's me," Jon said.

Bill grabbed his flashlight and turned it on. He shined it in the direction of the voice.

It was Jon, standing before him in the flesh. A hatchet hung by his side, and the gun was clenched underneath his arm. Bill relaxed, the anxiety torturing his soul easing.

"Oh, thank God. I thought you were dead, Jon," Bill said, stumbling to his feet.

"No, I'm here," Jon said. "I'm here." Jon ran toward Bill, dropping the gun from under his arm and smiling.

Bill sprinted toward Jon, hands outstretched and tears rolling down his cheeks. The two boys embraced and squeezed each other tight.

"They got Dup," Bill said through tears and sniffles.

"I know," Jon said. He was crying now. "I heard it all."

"Have you seen Terry or Matt?" Bill asked.

"No," Jon whispered. "I haven't seen them or heard them."

Bill broke the hug. "Do you think they are ... you know?"

"I don't know, Bill. I honest to God have no idea."

"I wish we would have never come out here."

"Me too," Jon said. "I am sorry I talked y'all into this. It's my fault they're dead!" Jon's body convulsed with sobs. "I'm so, so sorry!"

Bill embraced his best friend. "No, man, it's not," he said. "We came out here because we wanted to." He tucked Jon's head under his chin. "It's not your fault."

Jon buried his face into Bill's shoulder. "I killed them. It is my fault ... all my fault ... We should have just gone to the police."

Bill held his shaking friend, his warm tears soaking through his shirt. He pushed Jon away and gave him a gentle shake. "Hey, let's just focus on getting out of here, okay?"

"Okay," Jon said with a nod. He wiped his tears with the back of his arm. "Okay, but I gotta piss first."

"Yeah, me too," Bill said.

Jon walked a few yards over and stepped behind a tree to urinate. As he did, Bill thought he saw the hem of a black dress around Jon's feet.

Bill shook his head. "Just a long night." He turned around, unzipped, and let it flow. The boys listened as the sound of piss hitting leaves echoed in their ears. Bill finished up first and turned back around.

"You done yet, Jon?" he asked.

"Almost," Jon said.

Bill put his hands in his pockets and gazed up at the sky. He heard Jon zip up, then step from behind the tree.

"Now," Bill said. "Let's get out of here." He looked twice at Jon, blinking. "Jon, where the hell did you find that?" Bill pointed at the video recorder in Jon's hand.

Jon lowered his head, peering at Bill through a furrowed brow. An unusually large, awkward grin stretched across Jon's face. He bore his teeth—yellow, greenish, infected teeth.

"I'm not Jon, boy," Craddock's voice said.

Bill's eyes twitched while his brain tried to process what stood before him. Jon's grin widened all the way across his face, stretching back to his ears. His teeth protruded forward, elongating and coming to points at the ends. Jon's eyes burst with a loud pop. A watery liquid mixed with blood spewed out his sockets, the sound like a faucet running full blast. Sharp, black tips appeared in the eye sockets and extended outward. The horns snaked out, then curved to the top of his head. The ends of Jon's fingernails ripped open, and knifelike claws extended from the tips. His skin darkened to a charcoal gray, and its texture turned leathery. There was no more Jon, only the demon.

Panic rose in Bill again, slapping his senses like a brutal backhand. Jon was dead. Dup was dead. Terry and Matt were dead as well. Yes, they were all dead, and he was about to die too.

A fight took place inside of Bill as he processed it all. He could either bend over and take it up the ass from this dick-eating hellspawn or he could fight. Jon would have wanted him to be brave in his final minutes on this planet. Bill decided to go down swinging.

"What did you do to my friends, you fucking bastard?" Bill yelled, clenching his fists. "What did you do with Jon?"

"Oh," Craddock said. "This is Jon. I got him in here with me. I can't let him have control right now 'cause it's not time."

Rage. Fury. Wrath. They all awakened inside Jon like a rising phoenix. "Don't you fucking touch him, Craddock! Don't you make me do it! Let him go! Bill is my best friend!"

"I know," Craddock's voice said to Jon. "That is why I am gonna kill him."

Bill had an idea. You don't fight demons like

humans. You have to cast them out. He thought about The Exorcist. He remembered the old made-for-television movie The Demon Murder Case and how the demon was cast out by an exorcism. Determination arose inside of him. "This is the end of the line for you, Craddock. In the name of Jesus, I command you to let Jon go!"

The demon took a few steps towards Bill, tilting its head. "What, boy? What did you say to me? You some sort of exorcist now, huh? Father Bill, is that what I should call you?" The demon cackled. "Well, forgive the fuck out of me, Padre. Guess I'll just pack my goddamn bags and catch the next train back to hell." The demon snarled, saliva oozing down its chin. "I'll skull fuck you until my dick pops out the back of your head. Then I'll cum all over your brains and lap them up like miso fucking soup. Then I'll say boy, that Bill gives some good head!"

Bill took a step back, his determination and faith shot to shit. The demon lifted the camera and hit the record button.

"You think you can say some magic words and make me gone," Craddock said. "It would take one hell of an exorcism to get me out, boy, and you ain't got that in you."

"Craddock, let him go!" Jon demanded. He strained with all of his might to get his body back under his control, but his efforts were fruitless. "Fuck!" he yelled. All he could do was watch.

"You know what Jon is gonna do to you, Bill? Do you?" The demon crept closer.

Bill gave his head a slow shake.

"He is gonna bleed you dry, boy!"

"Fuck you," Bill said. "And you know what, Craddock?"

"What, you little cocksucker?"

"Your wrinkly old ass forgot about something."

"Fuck you, shit stain!" Craddock flipped Bill the bird.

"Fear doesn't work on a person when they know they're already dead!" Bill howled and charged at the demon.

The demon met Bill with a foot to the chest, sending his body thudding to the ground. Bill let out a loud huff, smacking his head on a large branch. Craddock jumped on top of him, holding down his arms with his knees and sitting on his chest.

The force of the blow and the sheer weight of the creature were too much for Bill to handle. He wheezed and gasped for air.

"Now, it's time to watch, Jonny boy," Craddock said to Jon. He lifted up the camera so Jon could see.

"No! No, no, no, no, no! Craddock, you asshole! Let us go!" Jon screamed. "Bill! Bill! Bill!"

"Jon ... Jon ...," Bill said between gasps. "Hard ... to ... breathe ..."

The demon's claw appeared in front of the lens. Jon watched as the razor-sharp nail pressed against Bill's throat.

Bill thought about his third birthday party. His dad had gotten him his first Big-Wheel that year. Then a memory from when he was five and his dad taught him how to hit off a tee. He remembered when he was seven and caught his first eight-pound bass. He held it up for his mom to take a picture of it. The photo was still framed and on his night stand.

Then there was the time he and Jon ate so much fried chicken they had terrible gas. His mom made him and Jon stay outside the rest of the day because they kept stinking up the house. He remembered how even though Jon didn't care for gangster rap, he would look at all the albums with him and listen to the songs Bill would recommend.

Bill didn't think he had any more tears left in him, yet here they were, bubbling forth. He cried over Terry and Matt. He cried over Dup. He cried over his mom and dad. But in his last moments, he cried over Jon the most.

"Jon," Bill wheezed. "I … I … I love y—"

Bill's last word was cut short by the claw of the demon slicing open his throat.

"Nonononononono! Oh God! No!" Jon screamed. "Bill! Bill! Goddammit! Bill! Why God! Why the fuck! Oh shit! Fucking hell!"

The demon cupped his hand under the wound, scooping Bill's blood and lapping it with his tongue. He moved the camera close to Bill's face so Jon could watch the life drain from his best friend's eyes.

"Bill," Jon said. "Do you remember that picture of

me in my 49ers gear and you in your Chicago Bulls? We had our arms around each other and we were smiling? That is us, man. Best buds and always happy together." Jon stared deep into Bill's eyes through the camera. The light in his friend's eyes faded.

"Bill, I remember the first time you came over and brought your wrestlers. We played all evening and then watched USA Up All Night," Jon said. "We both liked Rhonda's tits." He snickered. "Oh, and remember our boy band? That was some shit, wasn't it, buddy? Remember … Remember …" Jon couldn't hold it in anymore. He sobbed and wept, still trying to talk to his friend.

Jon heard his demon body slurping Bill's blood.

"Remember our first wrestling match we went to and I hit Greg the Hammer Valentine over the head with a poster holder?" Jon said. "He was like, hey, give me some fucking protection."

Jon paused, recounting more memories. "Remember when my dog Spacey died? You just sat there with me and let me hug you and cry … and now … oh God … and now all I want to do is hug you and hold you as you die!"

Bill's head went limp and fell to the side. The light had left his eyes.

"Bill? Bill?" Jon asked. Bill was dead, and there was nothing Jon could do about it but cry. "Bill! Oh, Bill! I am gonna miss you. You were my best friend … my best … friend …"

Jon sat as a prisoner in his own mind and body and

wept over his friend. The only sound he could hear besides his own weeping was his demon body still slurping Bill's blood.

9

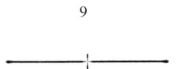

Jon Benson stood in a white room. It was so bright he couldn't tell where the floor ended and the walls began. Craddock was gone, and Jon's soul was bonded to his demon body. Before him stood a tree. It resembled a willow tree, but the branches were bare and much thicker. They snaked in and out of each other, and every so often, another branch seemed to come forth.

Theodosia was on one side of the tree, still dressed in her black dress. Standing on the other side of the tree, towering above all, was the Tetromet. He had a black goat skull for a head. His feline body was decorated with black and red stripes. His tail was that of a viper. The tip of his flaming sword dug into the floor, and his paws rested on the bone hilt.

"Jon," Theodosia said and stepped forward.

"Yes," Jon said.

"You are now a guardian demon. This means you will protect those the Tetromet has chosen to further his kingdom. You will teach them of his ways and about me, his prophetess. Do you understand?"

"I do," Jon said.

"Your first assignment is to protect your younger brother, Cyrus Benson," Theodosia said. "Tetromet has chosen him to help further his cause so more branches may be added to his tree." Theodosia reached out her wrinkled hand and caressed some of the branches.

"But, Theodosia," Jon said. "I don't have a younger brother. It's just me."

"Look and see," Theodosia said.

Jon went into a trance. He saw his parents mourning his death. The vision shifted to them commencing the act of sex, trying to replace what was lost—a son.

"You will soon, my child," Theodosia said. "Very, very soon."

"Who do I need to protect him from?"

"Cory," Theodosia said. "And other creatures from the Plane. You will be Cyrus's guardian demon."

The vision ended, and Jon stared at the tree. He saw more branches form. "As you wish, Theodosia. As you wish."

Jon left the Ethereal Plane. He now walked through his parents' bedroom. His mom and dad were sound asleep in their bed. Jon stood over his mother, shrouded in a cloak of darkness and unseen by the naked eye. Jon caressed her cheek with the back of his gray, leathery hand. "Sweet dreams, Mother. Sweet dreams. I won't let anything happen to you. Not to you or Cyrus." From then on, Jon stayed by his mother's side, waiting for her to give birth.

ABOUT THE AUTHOR

Ezekiel Kincaid is the author of numerous short stories and multiple books. His experience as a pastor, chaplain, and paranormal investigator brings a touch of reality to the twisted tales he weaves. He is also a writer for Mixed Alternative Magazine, where he talks about all things horror, and writes a monthly short story series for Godless called Southern Discomfort. He hosts two YouTube shows, Southern Discomfort and Immortal Shadows, that deal with the paranormal, horror, and spirituality. Ezekiel Kincaid resides in his hometown of Central, Louisiana, but longs to live in a haunted house somewhere along the East Coast. He's a huge fan of sarcastic humor, holds three theological degrees, and loves telling annoying dad jokes. One day, he hopes to own a 1980s Winnebago that he can decorate with creepy dolls.

Want more Tetromet and Theodosia? Check out these other titles from The Paranormal Pastor:

The Dreadful Death (3 book series)
The Door (Southern Discomfort Season 1 Issue 1)
Tetromet Rising (Southern Discomfort Season 1 Issue 4)
The Call of the Tetromet (Southern Discomfort Season 1 Issue 7)
The Tetromet (Southern Discomfort Season 2 Issue 3)
Bone Box (Godless Reads on YouTube)

ABOUT THE
PUBLISHER/EDITOR

———————|———————

Dawn Shea is an author and half of the publishing team over at D&T Publishing. She lives with her family in Mississippi. Always an avid horror lover, she has moved forward with her dreams of writing and publishing those things she loves so much.

Follow her author page on Amazon for all publications she is featured in.

Follow D&T Publishing at their website
dt-publishing.com,
or search for their Facebook Group

Or email here: dandtpublishing20@gmail.com

The Tetromet Tapes by Ezekiel Kincaid

Edited by Tasha Schiedel

Cover by Ash Ericmore

Formatting by Ash Ericmore

Printed in Great Britain
by Amazon

42061187R00106